"You were saying?"

Emma prompted Pres.

"It's like this," Pres said. "I really care for Sam, but these little games of hers are gettin' real tired."

"Sam is . . . afraid to be in love, I think," Emma said slowly.

"Maybe so," Pres acknowledged. "I don't want to tie her down—I don't want to tie myself down! But I want some honesty and some grown-up behavior."

"Me too!" Emma exclaimed. "I wish Kurt was more like you!" Emma clapped her hand over her mouth, and blushed a bright red. "I didn't mean that the way it sounded. . . ."

The SUNSET ISLAND series
by Cherie Bennett

Sunset
ON THE Road

CHERIE BENNETT

Virgin

First published in Great Britain in 1995 by
Virgin Books
an imprint of Virgin Publishing Ltd
332 Ladbroke Grove
London W10 5AH

First published in the USA in July 1991 by
The Berkley Publishing Group
published by arrangement with
General Licensing Company, Inc.

Printed and bound by
Cox & Wyman Ltd, Reading, Berks

ISBN 0 863 69955 3

A NOTE FOR BRITISH READERS FROM
THE PUBLISHERS

This story is set in the United States of America and has been
written in American English. We feel that the American
spelling, grammar and vocabulary that Cherie Bennett uses in
her writing are an important part of the story, and we haven't
changed anything that was in the original American edition.
Therefore, be warned: you will find in this book words,
phrases and spellings that are not usual, and sometimes
downright incorrect, in British English.

For Jeff, forever

ONE

"Tell me the truth," Sam begged Emma. "I look like dog meat, right?" Sam had on a black satin and lace bustier with a short see-through hot pink chiffon skirt over fishnet hose, and black cowboy boots encircled with a rhinestone ankle bracelet.

"Right," agreed Emma, who was wearing an identical outfit, but with an acid green skirt. She turned to the mirror and fixed her lipstick.

"Oh no! Oh God, I knew it!" Sam wailed, falling into the nearest chair. Tall and thin with wild red hair, Sam was naturally very small busted. "No girl with my figure should wear a bustier!" She looked down morosely at the black satin and lace bra cups of her bustier, which stuck out much further than the flesh underneath them. "A family of four could move in here."

Emma turned around to face her friend. She swept her perfect, straight blond hair away

1

from her heart-shaped face. "Sam, I was kidding. You look great."

"No, you weren't," Sam insisted, trying to produce cleavage by pressing her upper arms tightly against either side of her chest. "I'm hopeless."

"I've never seen you this nervous before!" Emma exclaimed.

"Well, we've never been in a huge Battle of the Bands before," Sam replied, still staring down at her chest. "There's a lot at stake here!"

"Yes, but it's not dependent on your bust line!" Emma said with a laugh.

"Very funny," Sam mumbled, finally giving up on the bustier. "I know what Carrie would say—it's my fault for not trying this stupid costume on before today. Then I would have had time to have the top altered—"

"—but as usual you put it off," Emma finished for her.

"Sue me, I'm not a real plan-ahead kind of babe," Sam muttered. She looked at Emma, whose bustier had been taken in to fit her snugly, and she sighed again.

"I love you just the way you are," Emma assured her, turning back to the mirror to finish getting ready.

"Might as well put on some more makeup," Sam said, moving over to the mirror. "Maybe it'll distract from what nature forgot."

Sam pulled out her matte red lipstick and carefully filled in her lips.

"Flirting With Danger, you're on in ten!" a voice from the hallway called.

"Hey, you guys!" Carrie Alden cried, running into the dressing room. She was a fresh-faced girl with brown hair, brown eyes and a curvy body, which was now hidden under an over-sized John Lennon T-shirt. "I came in to say break a leg!" She hugged Emma, then Sam. "You two look great!"

"Don't lie to me, Carrie Alden," Sam said darkly. She put one hand into the top of each bustier cup. "There's air where there should be me!"

Carrie scrutinized Sam. "I don't think it will even show from out in the crowd," she decided.

Sam's eyebrows shot up. "You're not going to tell me about how dumb I was not to try this on before today?"

"Well, now that you mention it . . ." Carrie teased.

"I am so pissed at myself!" Sam cried.

"Hey, I've got it!" Carrie exclaimed, her face lighting up. She reached inside her T-shirt.

"Don't tell me," Sam said dramatically. "Your breasts are detachable and you're lending them to me."

"Close," Carrie said. She pulled the shoulder pads out of her T-shirt and handed them to

3

Sam. "Stick these in your bustier. Instant cleavage!"

Sam looked doubtful, but she took Carrie's shoulder pads and arranged them, and then looked in the mirror. "Whoa baby!" she whooped. "It actually works!"

"Hubba-hubba," Emma opined with a laugh.

"Un-frigging-believable!" Sam exclaimed. "I'm a total babe-a-saurous!"

"Glad to be of help," Carrie said. She lifted the camera that hung around her neck and snapped off a candid shot of Sam admiring her reflection in the mirror.

"You saved the day, girlfriend," Sam told Carrie, giving her a hug. "I'm putting shoulder pads in all my clothes—and I don't mean on my shoulders!"

Carrie laughed and waved good-bye. "Do great!" were her final words.

"We will—now," Sam told Emma.

Emma just smiled, shook her head, and went back to finishing her makeup.

Feeling much better, Sam sat down in front of the mirror and picked up her mascara. She was a little embarrassed that she had freaked out over something as minor as her cleavage. *I mean, I'm the one who's supposed to be the professional,* she reminded herself. She knew it had to do with the fact that as a backup singer/dancer for Flirting With Danger—or The

Flirts, as they were commonly known to their fans—she always felt a little insecure standing next to the extremely gorgeous, extremely well-built, and extremely obnoxious third member of the backup trio—Diana De Witt. *Well, at least now I won't look like a boy next to her,* Sam thought with satisfaction.

As she stared at her reflection in the mirror, Sam thought about how far The Flirts had come—how far her own life had come in the past year.

The summer before she, Emma, and Carrie had all begun working as au pairs on beautiful, romantic Sunset Island, a resort island off the coast of Maine. They were as different as could be, and it seemed unlikely that they'd ever become friends. Carrie was from New Jersey, the daughter of two pediatricians who were very politically active. Emma was a Boston heiress, a true blue blood, who had been educated in Europe and spoke five languages fluently. And Sam was from the excruciatingly small farm town of Junction, Kansas—a town and a lifestyle she intended to leave far behind her forever.

Not only had the three become friends, they'd become best friends. *Maybe it's actually because of our differences that we're so close,* Sam mused. Well, whatever it was, they were now in their second summer together on the island,

and they were closer than ever. When push came to shove they were always there for each other. *And we always will be,* Sam told herself with satisfaction.

One of the most exciting things that had happened recently was that Sam and Emma had become backup singer/dancers for The Flirts. Carrie's boyfriend, Billy Sampson, was the lead singer and guitar player. Sam's boyfriend, Presley Travis, was the bass player. The Flirts had a huge local following, and were working night and day toward their dream of getting a recording contract.

When the guys decided to add backup singer/dancers, Sam (who had danced professionally at Disney World for a while) begged Emma and Carrie to audition with her. Carrie had refused, saying she was a much more behind-the-scenes type. And anyway, photography was her first love; she'd be taking pictures of the band. But to Sam's surprise, Emma had actually agreed to audition. And to Sam's even greater surprise, Emma had not only turned out to be really talented, but they'd both been hired.

That was the good news. The bad news was that Diana De Witt, their archenemy and one of the most obnoxious people ever to be put on the planet, had been picked as the third backup. Emma had gone to boarding school with Diana in Europe, and Diana really seemed to have it in for her, and now for Emma's friends, too. Diana had even had a brief affair the summer before with Kurt Ackerman, Emma's boyfriend—mostly just to prove that she could get him away from Emma. She was a barracuda of the first order.

I won't even think about Diana. She's not worth my time, Sam told herself, reaching for the hair spray. Tonight was a really important night for all of them. They were about to compete in the East Coast division of the big Battle of the Bands Contest, sponsored by *Rock On* magazine. The winning band would get five thousand dollars, and would tour as the opening act for the hot new rock star Johnny Angel. It was the opportunity of a lifetime, and they were all totally psyched.

Sam saw it as a stepping stone—*today a backup singer/dancer,* she told her reflection, *tomorrow a star.*

"My God, what did you do?" Diana demanded, coming up behind Sam and staring at Sam's enhanced reflection in the mirror. Diana was wearing a third version of their stage outfit— with a white chiffon skirt.

Sam stared back at Diana's reflection and made a face. She'd been so lost in thought, she hadn't even heard her come into the dressing room.

"What did you do, *grow* overnight?" Diana demanded.

"Shoulder pads," Sam told her smugly, cupping her hands underneath them. She was pleased to note that for once Diana did not outshine her in their low-cut outfits.

"Oh really," Diana said, narrowing her eyes at Sam's reflection. She looked thoughtful for a moment, then marched over to the corner of the room where her sweater was thrown over a chair. She pulled out two Velcroed shoulder pads and slipped them into her bustier.

"Uh, Diana," Emma said, eyeing her skeptically, "you don't exactly need those."

"I know," Diana said, tossing her chestnut curls and looking with satisfaction at her now more than formidable bust line. "But I look fabulous."

"You look like your cup runneth over," Sam told her dryly.

"Jealousy doesn't become you," Diana chided Sam.

"I'm just telling you the truth," Sam said. "It looks ridiculous."

"Oh really?" Diana said coolly. "Well, how about if I just go ask Pres how well he likes it?"

"Go do whatever the hell you want," Sam yelled. "I couldn't care less!"

"Sure," Diana said sarcastically. She fluffed her hair once in the mirror and turned to the door. "See you on stage, Olive Oyl," she told Sam over her shoulder, and sashayed out the door.

"What a lovely person," Emma said lightly. "So gracious. So giving."

"So dead," Sam added. "Because one of these days I'm really going to kill her."

"I'll help," Emma said.

"Flirting With Danger, places!" the stage manager yelled from the hall.

"This is it!" Sam cried, jumping up.

Emma stood up slowly, her face going white. "I think I just got really, really nervous."

"You'll be terrif," Sam assured her.

"This isn't like singing with the guys at the Play Café," Emma gulped, naming the local hangout on the island where they'd first sung with The Flirts. "This is . . . big!"

"Yeah," Sam agreed, going a bit pale herself. "Like five thousand big."

"Five thousand?" Emma whispered.

Sam nodded. "That's how many people Pres told me they were expecting."

"Oh, wow . . ." Emma breathed, falling back toward her chair.

"Uh-huh. We gotta go," Sam said, pulling Emma back to her feet. "Here's what we'll do. We'll both pretend we're your mother."

"My mother?" Emma said faintly.

"Right," Sam confirmed. "Your mother is the

9

snootiest woman I ever met in my life. She is never intimidated by anything."

"You mean she never lets it *show* that she's intimidated by anything," Emma corrected her.

"Exactly." Sam nodded. "Just like us."

"Right," Emma agreed. "I can do that. I think."

"Em, I've seen you do it a hundred times," Sam told her. "So, let's make it a hundred and one."

"You got it," Emma said firmly, as if she were trying to convince herself.

"Okay," Sam said, taking one last look at her reflection in the mirror, "time for you and me and my new set of headlights to rock and roll!"

"Are you having a good time?" the emcee yelled through the microphone to the crowd that filled Portland Municipal Auditorium.

"Yeahhhh!" the crowd roared back.

Behind the curtain, Flirting With Danger stood in their places, waiting for deejay Brucie Michaels—or Uncle Brucie, as he was known to his fans—to introduce them. One of the most famous deejays in rock, he even had his own show on MTV.

"Our next band is hot, and I do mean sizzling," Uncle Brucie rasped into the microphone in his distinctive voice.

Behind the curtain Emma quickly grabbed Sam's hand and squeezed hard. Sam squeezed back.

10

"From Sunset Island, Maine . . ." Uncle Brucie announced, "please welcome . . . Flirting With Danger!"

Some local fans began screaming, everyone applauded, and the curtains parted to reveal the band lit up by traveling strobe lights. Sly, the drummer, counted off with his sticks, and the guys began a hot rock riff.

"Hello, Portland!" Billy yelled into the microphone over the music, and the audience cheered. After four measures led by Billy's moaning guitar, he leaned back into the mike to sing their opening song, "Love Junkie."

> You want too much
> And you want too fast
> You don't know nothin'
> About making love last.
> You're a love tornado
> That's how you get your kicks
> You use me up
> And move on to your next fix. . . .
> You're just a Love Junkie
> A Love Junkie, baby
> A Love Junkie
> You're drivin' me crazy. . . .

"Love, love junkie, baby!" the girls sang into their microphones. At the end of the chorus they spun around and then went back into their

11

left-right sway, singing "oooh" into their mikes on the verse.

Billy played the final electric riff on the guitar, wailed the final lyric, then jumped up in the air on the last beat, and the whole band ended in perfect synchronicity.

The audience was on its feet, yelling and cheering!

"They love us!" Sam screamed to Emma.

Emma beamed back happily. *This is the most fun I ever had in my entire life,* she thought to herself. *I'm doing something most girls only dream of doing!*

"Thank you. Thank you very much," Billy said in a soft voice as the audience quieted down. "This next tune is for someone very special. . . ." The lights dimmed, until Billy was bathed in a pink spot. He looked down below him and there was Carrie with her camera, looking up at him and snapping his picture. "This is for you, Carrie," he added. Then he closed his eyes and sang a sweet, simple love song, "You Take My Breath Away."

The auditorium was hushed, the audience transported by Billy's sexy voice and the poignant lyrics of the tune he'd written for Carrie. Carrie smiled up at him, her heart completely filled with love. *How did I get so lucky?* she thought to herself, snapping another picture of Billy.

12

When Billy finished the final note, silence hung in the air a moment; then the crowd burst into applause.

"Thank you," Billy said into the mike. He waited for the applause to die down. "Thank you. For our last tune, I say we fire this place up!" Pres began a hot bass line as Billy was speaking. Sly came in on the drums. Jay began a catchy riff on the keyboards. "Are you ready to party?" Billy yelled out to the crowd.

"Yeah!" the crowd yelled.

"Then lemme hear you yell *'party!'*" Billy called.

"Party!" the crowd called in rhythm to the music.

"Party!" Billy sang again.

"Party!" the crowd yelled even louder.

"Okay ladies, do your stuff!" Billy called to the girls.

This was the moment before the lyrics to the final tune, "Wild Child," where Emma, Sam, and Diana were featured doing aerobic and gymnastic dancing. The girls ran forward, and while the guys played, they went into their dance.

Eat your heart out, Janet Jackson, Sam thought triumphantly, as she whirled around in a double pirouette.

Emma and Diana were on either side of her, and they both did single pirouettes in unison.

But when Diana whirled back around and went into the shimmy move on the offbeat, the top of her strapless bustier slipped down slightly. Her breasts were so compressed from the shoulder pads underneath them that just as she did her final dip, the right one popped free of the top of her bustier for all the world to see.

Sam heard a loud wolf whistle from the crowd, and from the corner of her eye she saw Diana quickly pulling her bustier back into place with one hand while executing the final move with the other. Emma was on the other side of Sam, so she couldn't see what had happened. On the very last spin, which took the girls back to their places behind their microphones, Diana actually winked at the audience, then danced back into place.

I hate the witch, but I gotta admire her nerve, Sam thought to herself, as Billy began to sing "Wild Child."

When the song finished, the crowd went wild. Diana blew kisses to the audience, as if she had planned to expose herself all along.

"Flirting With Danger! Let's hear it for 'em!" Uncle Brucie screamed into the mike over the cheering crowd, which then screamed even louder. The Flirts waved and ran offstage.

"Oh God, that was incredible!" Sam whooped, throwing herself into Pres's arms with exuber-

14

ance once they reached the backstage area. "Do you think we won?"

"I think we got a shot at it," Pres said, hugging Sam hard. He looked down at Sam's bustier curiously. "You look . . ."

"Bigger?" Sam finished for him. She reached into the bustier and pulled out the shoulder pads. "That's the first and last time for me," she vowed. "After what happened to Diana on stage, I want my anatomy to stay right where God put it!"

Pres threw his head back and laughed. "Girl, you are too much."

The Flirts had been the fifth and final band to perform, so while the upcoming touring schedules for some big East Coast bands were announced, the judges—from *Rock On* magazine and various record companies—voted.

"Okay everybody, the judges have just handed me their decision," Uncle Brucie said. "Can I get all five bands out on stage?"

"This is it," Emma whispered to Sam as they walked back out. The stage quickly filled up with the various band members, all of them trying to look cool. Emma could sense that they all felt pretty much like she did, though—nervous and hopeful.

"I gotta say, I think the bands this year were the best I've ever heard," Uncle Brucie said. "How about a hand for everyone?"

15

The audience clapped dutifully, but they were ready to hear the winner announced.

"In third place, winner of five hundred dollars, from Newport, Rhode Island—Goes To Eleven!" Five guys with long hair sauntered forward and shook Uncle Brucie's hand. There was light applause from the audience.

"In second place, winner of one thousand dollars, from Jersey City, New Jersey, The Shore Girls!" More applause. Four girls in miniskirts came forward and hugged Uncle Brucie.

"Well, either we won or we got shut out completely," Sam whispered to Emma.

Emma held up crossed fingers and closed her eyes as Uncle Brucie got ready to announce the winner.

"The winner of this year's *Rock On* magazine's Battle of the Bands for the East Coast receives five thousand dollars, a tour with Johnny Angel of Polimar Records, and a chance to compete in the national Battle of the Bands finals. And the winning band is . . . from Sunset Island, Maine . . . Flirting With Danger!"

Sam, Emma, and Diana began screaming, the crowd went nuts, and Uncle Brucie handed Billy a check and shook his hand.

"Bye, everyone. See you next year!" Uncle Brucie yelled, and the curtain came down on the stage.

Sam and Emma ran over to the side of the stage.

"We won! We won!" they screamed, jumping up and down together.

Sam stopped and held Emma at arm's length. "Do you realize what this means?"

Emma nodded. "We're going on tour!"

Sam screamed happily, "I'm gonna be a star!"

Carrie pushed her way backstage and ran over to her friends, hugging them both hard. "I am so happy for you guys!" she yelled.

"What about me?" Billy asked Carrie, tapping her on the shoulder.

Carrie turned around and put her arms around his neck, sliding her camera out of the way so she could hold him close. "You were wonderful," she told him softly.

"You'll come on the tour, won't you?" Billy asked her, pushing some of his long hair behind one ear.

"You betcha," Carrie assured him. "I'm sure I'll get some great photos."

"If I ever let you out of the hotel room," Billy murmured to her sexily.

Sam and Emma overheard Billy, and looked at each other. Were Billy and Carrie going to share a room on the road?

"Hey, I just realized something," Sam said to Emma. "If I room with you, and if Carrie

17

doesn't want to share a room with Billy, then she'll have to room with Diana."

Emma looked from Diana—who was busy flirting with the lead singer of Goes To Eleven—back to Billy, who was kissing Carrie. "No contest," Emma said flatly.

"I agree," Sam said. "As for me, I plan to make the finest guys in America ecstatic as we cross our happy land."

"What about Pres?" Emma asked as they headed back to the dressing room.

"I plan to make him happy, too," Sam said, lifting her hair off her sweaty neck.

"You are one of a kind, Sam," Emma said with a laugh.

"True," Sam agreed blithely. "And soon I'll be rich, famous, *and* one-of-a-kind! Now, ain't life grand?"

TWO

"Okay, listen up," Billy Sampson said, putting down the can of Pepsi he was drinking and leaning forward in his easy chair.

The rest of The Flirts, including Sam, Emma, and Diana, had been lazing around the living room of the house that Billy, Pres, and the other guys in the band shared, recalling the events of the Battle of the Bands two days earlier. They quieted down immediately. This was the meeting where they would begin to make the tour plans.

Emma still could not believe her luck. *It wasn't so long ago that I wasn't even in this band—and never even considered that I could be, for that matter,* she thought to herself. *Now here I am, going out on tour with one of the hottest young acts in the country!* Emma, who had toured the world and seen everything, had to admit that this was one adventure she had never even thought of having. And she expected

19

it would be nothing like anything else she'd ever done.

"I'm passing out the itineraries that *Rock On* faxed to me this morning," Billy said, handing out some papers.

"Mondo-official!" Sam said happily, looking down at her schedule.

"Let's try to get this meeting over with quickly," Billy said. "As far as I'm concerned, practicing for this tour is more important than getting bogged down in the business end."

"Right," Pres agreed. "This touring stuff is a whole new ball game. I've been through it before, and I've seen how success can mess up friendships. Really good friendships, even," he added seriously.

"Well, that's no problem," Diana said flippantly. "I can't stand *them* already!" She pointed her finger at Sam and Emma.

"Ditto," Sam shot back at her.

Pres ignored them. "First of all, me, Billy, Sly, and Jay had to decide whether to let you girls vote on band decisions," he said, in his Tennessee drawl.

"Band decisions?" Diana De Witt asked archly. "Such as—"

"Such as how to handle the tour, what tunes to do, that kind of thing," Sly Smith, the band's skinny drummer explained seriously.

"I knew *that*," Diana said haughtily. "I wasn't

born yesterday. I'm in the band, so obviously I'm voting."

"No, you're not," Billy said in an even voice.

"Of course I am," Diana said.

"Not in this band," Pres contradicted her. "The band is the four guys. You, Sam, and Emma sing backup."

"Wait a second," Sam said. "Since when isn't singing backup part of the band?"

"It's a fair question," Billy said, "so I want you to understand the decision. We were a band a long time before we added backup singers, and we'd be a band if you guys quit. So, the three of you are employees—that's how we figure it."

"But that's sexist!" Diana De Witt protested.

"I agree!" Sam yelled.

Emma stifled a laugh. Sam and Diana were actually arguing on the same side of an issue? And Diana De Witt was protesting because a guy was being sexist? *Sexist?* Emma marveled. *Diana De Witt is the world's biggest flirt and makes fun of any girl or woman not wearing perfect makeup and the latest clothes. What a crock!*

"We're not a democracy," Sly said pointedly.

"You weren't winning Battles of the Bands before you got us!" Diana shot back.

"True," Pres agreed. "And that's why we decided that we are open to opinions and will

21

take them into consideration; but the final decisions are ours."

"That is so totally not fair!" Diana seethed, flipping a wave of hair behind her ear.

"Maybe not," Pres said, "but that's the way it's going to be."

"Well, all I have to say," Sam said coolly, "is that one day I won't be a mere 'employee,' as you so quaintly put it, because I will have quit to form my own band!"

"Knock yourself out," Sly muttered, rolling his eyes.

"Now that that's clear," Billy said, giving Sly a sharp glance and retaking control of the meeting, "let's talk about the tour. First of all, we're going to need a road manager."

Emma was puzzled. "A road manager?" she asked.

Sly rolled his eyes and buried his scraggly-haired head in his pale hands.

"Get a grip, Sly," Sam snapped, catching what he did. "You're lucky to be in the same room as Emma."

Emma saw a deep crimson spread up Sly's neck.

"Time out!" Billy Sampson said, with real anger in his voice. He looked closely at each member of the band in turn, saying nothing, letting them know that he was truly irritated.

Finally he spoke. "We're leaving on tour in

just a few days. You girls haven't done it before, but we have. This meeting has gotten off to a crappy start. If we can't get along here, what's it gonna be like on the road?"

"Sorry," Sly said, but Emma could see he hardly meant it.

"Say it again," Billy told him. "You too, Sam."

Sam sighed. "Sorry," she said.

"Me, too," Sly said honestly. "Sometimes I'm too serious about this stuff. Sorry, Emma."

Emma managed a small smile. "It's all right," she said graciously.

"We were discussing a road manager," Billy reminded them. "That's the guy—person—who makes sure that we're where we're supposed to be when we're supposed to be there, and who handles the travel arrangements, hotels, pay-checks, press . . . that sort of stuff."

"Sounds like fun," Emma said.

Pres laughed. "It's the worst job in the world," he drawled. "All pain, no gain. No one notices you unless you mess up."

"And we need a roadie too, don't forget," Jay Bailey, the mild-mannered, bespectacled key-board player put in. Emma thought he looked a lot like a young James Taylor.

"I haven't," Billy sighed. "But it'll cost money. In our case, the road manager is gonna have to double as the roadie. Anybody know anybody with brains *and* muscles?"

23

"Who wants to work for crap pay?" Sly added morosely.

"Isn't *Rock On* magazine paying for everything?" Sam asked.

"Yeah," Billy confirmed. "But they pay us a certain amount of money for the whole band, and it doesn't matter if we have three people or ten people in the group, it's the same lump sum. In our case, we've got four musicians—"

"And three 'employees'," Sam added.

"Which makes seven people already," Billy continued, ignoring Sam's dig. "So a road manager—roadie—whatever we call him—his or her check is coming out of that same lump sum."

"In other words," Pres said, "we're not gonna make a fortune out of this deal."

But maybe we will *become famous,* Sam thought to herself.

"On the other hand," Sly said, "the dude's gotta be somebody really smart, trustworthy, hard-working—"

"How about Kurt?" Emma suggested impetuously.

Diana leaned toward Emma, exposing the top of her impressive cleavage. "Are you sure you'd want Kurt to go out on a tour that I'm on?" she asked Emma coyly.

"I'm not worried about you, Diana," Emma said lightly, though the fact that Diana had seduced Kurt the summer before was now very much on her mind.

"Not a bad idea," Billy said, looking around at the other members of the band for confirmation. They were all nodding their heads. They all knew Kurt Ackerman and knew that he was both smart and level-headed, and strong.

"He could handle it," Pres said slowly. "You think he'd be interested?"

"Kurt's interested in going anywhere Emma goes," Sam put in.

"If he can arrange his schedule," Emma said, "I think he'll love the idea."

"Any other suggestions?" Billy asked.

There were none.

"Okay Emma," Billy said, "you're nominated to ask him to do it. Two-fifty a week plus hotel. Just like you'll be making."

"Yowza!" Sam exclaimed. "Two hundred and fifty big ones a week! I'm rich!" *Compared to au pairing, that is.*

"It's only a two-week tour," Emma pointed out to her friend.

"What are you guys making?" Diana asked Billy.

"None of your business," Billy replied to her with a smile.

"Not enough to cover what it costs us to get there," Jay said, "I'll promise you that."

The money doesn't really matter to me, Emma

thought, *but it'll matter a lot to Kurt. And I think, all things considered, the guys are being very fair. They've obviously given all this careful thought.*

"What'll I tell Kurt his hours are?" Emma queried.

Billy smiled. "Standard hours for a rock and roll tour," he replied. "Meaning twenty-four hours a day, seven days a week. No sick days, no vacation."

"Does he get groupies at least?" Sam asked.

"Ain't no time for that nonsense," Pres drawled. "The road manager works harder than anyone."

"What does that mean," Sam asked Pres, "that you'll have time for groupies but Kurt won't?"

"Now, sweetmeat," Pres drawled, "why ride a pickup when I got me a Cadillac?"

Sam winced. "Was that pitiful car analogy supposed to be about me?"

Pres just grinned his lazy grin at her. Sam rolled her eyes.

"I'll talk to Kurt this afternoon," Emma promised eagerly. "I have a great feeling about this!"

"He said yes!" Emma exclaimed happily to Sam, sliding into the now-familiar booth under one of the many video monitors at the Play

Café. It was later that day, and the girls had planned to meet to talk about the big tour.

"All right!" Sam cried, shoving three french fries into her mouth from the half-devoured plateful in front of her. "Did you call Billy and Pres?"

"Right away," Emma replied, grinning. "Actually, Kurt called Billy."

"So, how'd you talk him into it?" Sam asked, reaching for her Coke. "Drop your drawers?"

"No," Emma said. "He just really wanted to do it!"

"Probably because he thinks you're finally *going* to drop your drawers out there at some swank-o hotel," Sam decided.

"Wrong again," Emma said smugly. "He loves me and he wants to be with me. Besides, this is something he'll be really good at!"

"So how did he get out of teaching swimming at the club and driving his taxi for two weeks?" Sam asked, dipping the last french fry into a glob of ketchup.

"He's the world's greatest employee," Emma explained. "I mean, he never asks for time off. He's got vacation time coming."

"Cool," Sam said. "It's going to be wild."

A harried-looking waitress came over, and Emma ordered a small green salad and a glass of iced tea. Sam took the opportunity to ask for another order of fries.

"What I want to know is how do you subsist

on that rabbit food you eat?" Sam asked, wrinkling her nose.

"What I want to know is why you don't weigh three hundred pounds." Emma laughed. A familiar figure caught her eye at the front door. "There's Carrie!"

Carrie waved and made her way through the crowd.

"Check this out!" Carrie cried, holding the sides of a red satin jacket. She twirled around in a circle. Though the front looked like a plain baseball jacket, when Carrie twirled around Emma and Sam saw the back had an embroidered black emblem on it:

FLIRTING WITH DANGER

EAST COAST TOUR

Sponsored by *Rock On* Magazine

Under the emblem was the Flirting With Danger logo of a guy holding a guitar in one hand, sitting on top of a speeding missile as if it were a bucking bronco.

"Tour jackets?!" Sam screeched. "Are we getting actual tour jackets?"

"Maybe . . ." Carrie said mysteriously, sliding into the booth.

"Take it off. It's now mine!" Sam ordered Carrie.

"Nope," Carrie replied, playfully slapping Sam's hands away. "Get your own."

"From where?" Emma asked.

"How did you get one?" Sam demanded.

"Connections," Carrie said smugly, a huge grin on her face.

"It's because she's sleeping with the leader of the band," Sam said confidentially to Emma.

"I am not sleeping with him!" Carrie exclaimed. A bunch of kids at the next table stopped to stare at her, and Carrie blushed. She leaned in toward her friends. "I am not sleeping with him," she repeated in a lower voice.

"Yet," Sam added.

"Yet," Carrie agreed mischievously. "Anyway, there are jackets for both of you. Billy's got them."

"Outrageous!" Sam cried. "My first tour jacket. It'll go in the museum!"

"Museum?" Emma asked, dubiously.

"When I'm rich and famous," Sam explained.

"Ah." Emma nodded.

"In Kansas," Carrie played along.

"Junction, Kansas," Emma said.

"Major tourist attraction," Carrie added.

"The biggest," Emma said.

"It's gonna be called Samland," Sam retorted,

29

outlining an invisible marquee with her hands. "They'll forget all about Graceland."

"How'd the jackets get made so soon?" Emma asked. "We only just won the contest."

"*Rock On* rush-ordered them," Carrie explained.

"Cool," Sam said. "I love it! Picture me and Pres in the moonlight, me wearing nothing but this tour jacket and a wicked grin. . . ."

"You talk so big," Carrie laughed, "but we know the real Sam."

"Well, don't say it too loud," Sam admonished her. "You'll ruin my reputation as the bad girl of Sunset Island."

"Sweet, innocent you?" Carrie asked, fluttering her eyelashes.

"Hey, speaking of sweet and innocent," Emma said, looking at Carrie. "We heard Billy asking you to share a hotel room with him on the tour."

"What did you tell him?" Sam asked. "I want the true dirt, word for word."

"Well—" Carrie began, just as the harried waitress came over to the table with Emma and Sam's food.

"I hope you're not planning to order now," she told Carrie.

"Just bring me a diet Coke when you get a chance," Carrie told her, and the waitress hurried away.

"You were saying?" Sam coaxed Carrie.

"I said I'd have to think about it," Carrie replied honestly.

"Well, you've got your choice," Sam told her. "If you don't room with him, you have to room with Diana De Bitch. Hmmmm. Tough choice!"

"Time out!" Carrie cried. "Maybe *you* should share with Diana, Sam."

"Wrongamundo," Sam answered breezily. "Just think of it as incentive."

"For what?" Carrie asked.

"Billy," Sam said lightly. "I mean, you gotta figure on any given night there'll be at least two people in Diana's room anyway. And both of them will be in her bed."

"Billy didn't put any pressure on you, did he, Carrie?" Emma asked softly.

"Not a bit," Carrie admitted. "All he said was that he loved me very much and would love it if I wanted to stay with him on this tour."

"Wow," Sam said. "And you told him you'd think about it?"

"Uh-huh," Carrie said.

"You want my opinion?" Sam asked.

"I think I'm going to get it anyway." Carrie grinned.

"It's in two parts," Sam replied.

"Part one?" Emma prompted her.

"You'd be a fool if you don't sleep with him," Sam answered.

31

"Wonderful advice from the oldest living virgin from the state of Kansas," Carrie said dryly. "And part two?"

"You'd be an even bigger fool if you sleep in the same room as Diana De Witt," Sam said, picking up her empty glass and banging it on the table like a gavel. "Case closed."

"Uh-uh," Carrie said, shaking her head in the negative. "The case is not closed. I'm not sleeping with Billy unless I decide I'm really, truly ready to sleep with Billy."

"Good," Emma agreed.

"Okay, okay," Sam said reluctantly. "But I don't see why you have to be so nauseatingly mature about all this."

"I'm so glad you approve," Carrie said sweetly. "I'll just make sure the hotel moves a cot for me into your room!"

THREE

The next day, Billy assembled the whole band, plus Carrie and Kurt, at his house, and had them all pile into the panel van that The Flirts used to get from gig to gig.

"Secret trip," he said, when Emma asked him where they were going.

"We're going to the mainland," Pres added, "and that's all we're going to tell you."

Billy drove them all to the ferry, and they caught the one o'clock boat to Portland. Once there Billy drove for about an hour south to Portsmouth, New Hampshire, before he finally pulled into a broken-up driveway. It looked to Emma like they were in the middle of nowhere.

"We're here!" Billy said.

"Where's here?" Sam asked, as she climbed out of the back of the van and stretched her cramped muscles.

"You'll see," Sly said maddeningly.

"Y'all wait here," Pres instructed, and Emma

watched him and Billy go up to the front door of the run-down house and ring the bell.

A medium-sized guy in his late twenties answered the door. He was wearing a black leather jacket and black jeans, and had dark hair that hung down way past his shoulders. Emma saw Pres and Billy talk with him a moment. The guy nodded and then motioned to Pres and Billy to follow him around to the back of the house.

"Y'all coming?" Pres said to the rest of them.

"This is not an amusing game," Diana said, brushing a speck of dirt off her white jeans.

Emma, Carrie, Sam, and Kurt looked at each other and shrugged. "Might as well," Sam said. They all followed Pres, Billy, and the long-haired guy to the back of the house.

There in the yard a bus was parked. An honest-to-God tour bus. While the guys conferred with the long-haired guy, the girls studied the bus—sleek metal sides, very few windows. Painted on the side of it were the words DARK HORSE BAND: RUNNING ON EMPTY. Carrie, who was never without her camera, snapped off a few pictures.

After some animated conversation Billy excused himself and came back to the girls.

"What do you think?" Billy asked them, grinning.

"Whose bus is that?" Sam exclaimed.

34

"His," Billy said, cocking his head toward the long-haired guy in the black leather jacket. "Chino Gimble's. You know him?"

They all shook their heads.

"He had a band named Dark Horse Band a few years back," Billy explained. "It's not a band any longer."

"What happened?" Carrie asked.

"They stopped selling records," Billy said with a shrug. "It happens."

"So they're not touring any more?" Diana queried.

"They're not a band anymore," Billy replied.

"But they have a bus," Sam said.

"No," Billy replied. "We have a bus."

A tour bus. I'm going to be riding around in a real tour bus, going from gig to gig, just like a rock star. I can't believe it, Sam thought with excitement. *This is like something on television. No, it's better than television, because it's actually happening to me!*

"You're actually buying it?" Emma asked eagerly.

"You got it," Billy answered.

"It better have air conditioning," Diana said, swatting a mosquito on her arm.

"How much is it?" Carrie queried, always practical.

Billy grimaced. "More than we can really afford, but hey, we just won five thousand

35

dollars! Besides, we don't have to pay it all at once."

"Well, I think it's fabulous," Sam said, slipping on her leopard-print sunglasses. "I'm totally psyched."

"Me too," Billy admitted with a grin. "Go in and take a look around. You're gonna be seeing a lot of it."

Emma saw Sam scramble up into the bus, and she and Carrie followed close behind. Before she could even get up the stairs, Emma heard Sam let out a war whoop.

"This is awesome!" Sam yelled. "We're stars!"

Emma got into the bus. It was like something out of a rock and roll documentary. The front part, besides having a semi-enclosed area for the bus driver, had two couchlike seating areas complete with tables, a video monitor and a CD sound system, and a small restroom. There was even a refrigerator and stove!

The girls made their way to the rear, exclaiming over everything they saw. They stepped through a dividing curtain into an area where sleeping lofts could accommodate eight people.

Emma felt someone come up behind and put his hands on her shoulders.

"What do you think?" Kurt said, nuzzling Emma's neck and grinning broadly.

"I think it's amazing," Emma replied happily,

sitting down on one of the loft beds. "Is this where we sleep between shows?"

"Girlfriend, you are ignorant to the ways of rock and roll," Sam chided her. "We don't sleep here! This is for catching a few zzz's."

"Then where?" Emma asked.

"Hotels," Kurt answered, pulling out a black loose-leaf notebook, and checking it carefully.

"What's that?" Sam demanded.

"A tour book," Kurt replied. "We've got basically the whole tour here."

Sam craned to see, but Kurt feinted away with the book.

"Uh-uh," he scolded her, "this is confidential stuff."

"C'mon," Sam begged. "I'll be your best friend."

"Forget it," Kurt said with a laugh. "Your job is to be great on stage; my job is to take care of all the details offstage. Now, where were we? Ah yes, hotels." He flipped to a section of the notebook.

"Well?" Sam asked eagerly. "Five star or what?"

Kurt grinned. "Five star, you got it," he answered. "Five star Holiday Inns. Hot and cold running water most days."

"Hey, I love Holiday Inns! It'll be a huge step up from living with the monsters!"

Kurt and Emma laughed. Sam was referring

to Allie and Becky Jacobs, the precocious twin fourteen-year-olds she took care of on the island.

"I love this!" Carrie cried, sticking her head between the curtains.

"Kind of small, isn't it?" Diana asked, pushing past Carrie.

"I think it's great," Billy said, walking up to Carrie. "And we're lucky to get it."

"Well, small isn't necessarily bad," Diana said lasciviously, staring at Billy through lowered lids. "Small can be . . . cozy. Intimate. You know."

"Chino asked if we want to take it for a spin," Billy said, ignoring Diana's flirtation. "I told him we might want to."

"Might?!" Sam cried. "Let's motor!"

"Not so fast," Billy answered. "You got a commercial driver's license?"

"Uh, no, but—" stammered Sam.

"Then who's going to drive?" Billy asked in a teasing voice.

"I will," Kurt spoke up. "I got a school bus driver's license last year."

"Kurt will!" Sam shouted triumphantly.

"Well, that's convenient," Billy said with a grin. "Actually, Jay has one, too, from his days as a roadie."

"Don't remind me," Jay called from behind them.

"Well, it means you two can take turns driving at least," Billy explained. He looked over at Kurt. "You want the first crack behind the wheel?"

"Absolutely!"

"Then let's go," Billy declared, reaching into his pocket and pulling out a key.

The whole group made their way up to the front of the bus, where Chino was sitting with Sly and Jay.

"We got someone with a commercial license," Billy said to Chino, as they piled onto the circular couch.

"Then let 'er rip," Chino said laconically, reaching into a bag and pulling out a video. He popped the video into the VCR under the monitor and pushed a few buttons. Instantly the cabin of the bus was filled with the sounds of metal rock, and a wild-looking band filled the video screen.

"What band is that?" Emma asked Chino, as Kurt started up the bus.

"Oh, just some band that used to be sort of famous," Chino replied in a flat voice.

Then Emma recognized the guitar player on the video monitor. It was Chino Gimble.

"Hey, it's you—" Sam began.

"Come on, crank this mother!" Chino yelled up to Kurt. "Let's rock and roll!"

Quickly Chino turned his face away from the

others, but not before Emma saw the edge of a tear slide down his leathery cheek. It dropped onto his black jeans.

It's all over for him, Emma thought to herself. *It must be so hard for him to sell this bus to us. Here his bus is going on the road again and he knows that he's not going with it.*

"Rock and roll," Chino murmured as he stared out the window. For him it was an ending, but for everyone else on the bus, it was all just beginning.

"Diana," Sam said, trying hard not to yell, "we are not wearing see-through bras on stage, and that's final!"

"Why Sam," Diana replied, "do I detect a touch of defensiveness in your voice?"

It was the next afternoon, and Sam, Emma, and Diana were in Camille's Collar, a lingerie/ costume shop on Congress Street in Portland. They'd been sent there by Billy and Pres with instructions to pick out and purchase a new set of stage outfits for the tour.

In Emma's opinion, the afternoon was not going at all well. Every suggestion that Sam had for outfits was instantly shot down by Diana, and every outfit that Diana proposed seemed to emphasize maximum exposure of her own bust line, which drove Sam crazy.

"I agree with Sam," Emma spoke up, finally.

"We want the audience to concentrate on the music, not on us."

"Get a grip, Emma," Diana scoffed. "Even you aren't that naive. You notice The Flirts didn't pick three fat, zit-infested, greasy-haired uggos to sing backup. We're supposed to look hot!"

"Did you ever hear about beauty shining from within?" Emma asked Diana, wincing at the incredibly crude remark.

"Yeah, sure," Diana snorted. "When's the last time you saw a tubbo on MTV?"

"Don't bother trying to have an intelligent conversation with her," Sam suggested. "She's a mental midget."

"Look who's talking," Diana flung back at Sam.

"The two of you are rapidly retrogressing," Emma said, "and it is giving me a headache. Can we please try a different store? We're not getting anywhere here."

"Suit yourself," Diana replied haughtily. She picked up her pocketbook, put her white jean jacket back on and headed for the door. Emma and Sam followed her.

"Where do you suggest, Emma?" Diana asked, making it obvious from her tone of voice that no idea of Emma's would suit her.

"Jane told me there's an interesting clothing store called Retro on this street," Emma proposed. Emma was referring to Jane Hewitt, the

41

lawyer whose kids she cared for on the island. "We passed it on the block just before this one."

"Retro?" Diana asked dubiously, her hands on her hips.

"Let's try it," Sam said firmly, leading the way down the street.

"Why not?" Diana said. "No matter where we go, Sam'll have the same problem."

"Yeah, you," Sam muttered under her breath.

They walked one block down Congress Street to a storefront that was covered in rock and roll posters from the 1960s, advertising shows by such groups as the Grateful Dead and Big Brother and the Holding Company at venues like the Fillmore and the Family Dog. The sound of loud classic rock music poured onto the street through the door.

"This is a joke, right?" Diana asked.

"See, you don't even know what's hip," Sam told Diana coolly. "Didn't you ever hear that everything old gets new again?"

"You are seriously brain damaged," Diana replied.

"Let's just try it," Emma said, leading the way into the store.

The interior of Retro was exactly as the storefront indicated—rock posters everywhere, black lights, psychedelic artwork, and loud music. And most of all, everywhere they looked clothes from the sixties and seventies filled the racks. And there was a section devoted exclusively to shoes.

"Gee. Far-out. Right on," Diana said sarcastically, flashing a peace symbol with two fingers.

Over by the lone cash register were two women in hippie attire standing together. They nodded at the girls but didn't move a muscle.

"So?" Diana asked Emma. "What now?"

I'm not sure what to make of this place, Emma thought to herself. *But no way am I going to admit that to Diana.*

"We look!" Emma said gaily, marching over to one of the racks filled with velour dresses.

"I draw the line at hip-hugger bell-bottoms," Sam said, gingerly pawing through the dresses with Emma.

"I could, like, help you, if you want," one of the saleswomen yelled over the blaring rock music. She ambled over to Sam and Emma. The woman appeared to be in her mid-forties, with a gray braid that reached down to her waist. She wore a tie-dyed T-shirt without a bra, a long skirt, and Birkenstock sandals. "On the other hand, it's cool if you don't want me to, like, intrude."

"You're not intruding," Emma assured her. "We're looking for stage costumes."

"Stage costumes," the woman repeated, sounding slightly stoned. "Cool."

43

"For a tour!" Sam shouted, over the loud music. "A rock and roll tour!"

"Oh yeah?" the woman said. "Far out. Would you like some herb tea?"

"This is some kind of a joke, right?" Diana asked.

"Oh, it's cool if you don't like herb tea," the woman said. "I'm Cinderella, but you can call me Cinda."

"It's definitely a joke," Diana decided.

"Gee, we don't have time for tea," Sam said, edging away from the woman.

"It will help your karma," the woman said. She glanced meaningfully at Diana. "You appear to need it."

"Well, Cinda," Emma said, "I think we'll pass on the tea. Maybe you can help us with the costumes."

"I doubt it," Diana mumbled under her breath.

"What kind of music do you play?" Cinda asked.

"Rock and roll," Sam yelled. Just then the music stopped. "Of course," Sam added, happy to be able to hear the sound of her own voice.

"Of course," Cinda repeated serenely. "But rock and roll like Jimi Hendrix or rock and roll like Black Sabbath?"

"Rock and roll like Flirting With Danger,"

44

Diana shot back, looking pointedly at her watch. "Can we get on with this?"

A smile crossed Cinda's face. "Well, why didn't you say so before?" Cinda said, grinning brightly. "The Sunset Island bad boys, isn't it? With Billy Sampson?"

All three girls were astonished that Cinda knew their band. It seemed as if she wouldn't have heard a record cut after the seventies.

"How do you know us?" Diana asked, pointedly.

"I didn't know there were girls in the group," Cinda responded. "But you must be backup singers."

"And dancers," Sam added. "We dance, too."

"Far out," Cinda said. "The guys have added yin to their yang. Very balanced. What sign are you?"

"I mean it, I am out of here in two minutes," Diana threatened.

"Her system must be very backed up," Cinda said. She turned to Diana. "Have you considered a high colonic?"

Sam burst out laughing. "I told you Diana was full of it!"

"I believe I have just the thing for you." Cinda grinned. "Wait here."

She dashed off into a back room, and returned in an instant carrying three identical white boxes.

"Check these out," Cinda said, opening the boxes. "They used to belong to some friends of mine who toured with Herman's Hermits."

"Herman's whose?" Sam asked.

Emma shushed her, reached over, and took one of the boxes. She held up what was inside: an all-white, all-fringe, sleeveless nylon mini-dress with a round neckline.

"Whoa, baby!" Sam cried. "Seriously retro!"

"Thank you," Cinda said serenely.

Diana took the dress from Emma. "I almost kind of . . . like this," she admitted. "You think these will fit us?" she asked Cinda.

"Oughtta," Cinda said. "If not, I sew."

"Let's try 'em!" Sam shouted. She grabbed one and headed for the dressing room.

"What size shoes do you guys wear?" Cinda asked, as the three of them took the boxes into the dressing room.

The girls shouted their sizes to Cinda, then went in to try on the dresses. They sorted out the sizes, each finding one that more or less fit, or would with a little alteration.

"Bizarre," Diana said, shaking her fringed torso at the mirror. "Did you ever see this old show—they show it on cable sometimes—*'Hootenanny!'*"

"Yeah, that's it!" Sam cried. "The dancers dressed just like this!"

46

"It's kind of fun," Emma said, turning around to look at herself from behind.

Cinda stuck her head into the dressing room.

"Try these," she suggested. She handed them each a pair of white patent leather go-go boots in their correct size.

"Go-go boots!" Sam yelled with a laugh. "This is hilarious! My mom used to wear these in junior high school or something!"

"Probably." Cinda grinned. "But they'll look better on you with those dresses."

The girls added the go-go boots to their ensembles, and stood together in front of the full-length mirror appraising themselves.

"Girls," Sam said, "I wouldn't believe it if I didn't see it with my own eyes."

"You're right," Diana added, nodding her head.

"You think?" Emma asked.

"I know," Sam replied. "Flirting With Danger's three dangerous backup singers have found themselves a look!"

"You're wearing *what*?" Kurt asked, as he sat with Emma on the main pier on the ocean side of the island. Emma had met Kurt there as they'd planned earlier in the day, and the two of them were talking on one of the pier's many benches.

"White fringe minidresses with go-go boots."

Emma grinned, trying to get used to the idea herself.

"You're kidding," Kurt said.

"I'm not," Emma replied, leaning against Kurt. " I love it too!"

"I never figured you to be the go-go boots type," Kurt said with a smile.

"Me neither," Emma agreed. "I guess I'll leave my tasteful pearls at home when I wear that little number."

"Are you planning to send your mother photos?" Kurt asked dubiously.

"From the neck up." Emma laughed.

"Well, one good thing," Kurt said, as he held Emma close.

"What's that?" Emma asked softly.

"That we'll be together—really together—for two whole weeks," Kurt explained. "That's kind of a record for us."

"I'm looking forward to it," Emma murmured into his neck.

"Not as much as I am," Kurt replied huskily.

"Don't be so sure," said Emma, as she turned her lips up to Kurt's.

He kissed her very gently, first on the lips, then on the cheek, then on her eyelids, and then on her lips again.

"Heavenly," Emma said. "I like that. A lot."

"Me too," Kurt said. "And to think I'll see you

every day for fourteen days wearing white go-go boots—how will I be able to control myself?"

"Willpower," Emma said with a grin. "Anyway, we don't wear those outfits every night—they are only one of our many looks."

"What are your other looks?" Kurt asked.

"That's what we're trying to figure out," Emma said with a shrug. "Anyway, the retro outfits will be fun. It's a nice change from the skimpy, sexy numbers we usually wear. It's overkill."

"I disagree," Kurt said teasingly. "I love those skimpy, sexy numbers on you."

"Oh really?" Emma teased him right back. "Well, from what I hear, you'll probably be too busy to appreciate them."

"Emma, trust me," Kurt said. "I could never be *that* busy."

"Wouldn't it be funny if this turned out to be something you loved doing?" Emma asked Kurt. She ran her fingers through his hair. "Maybe it'll turn out to be a whole career for you."

"Hey Emma, come on. You know the only reason I'm doing this is to be with you."

For some reason Emma couldn't define, that comment made her feel very uncomfortable. "But maybe you'll end up liking the work anyway," she said.

"Being a roadie?" Kurt said dubiously. "No thanks!"

"Being a road manager," Emma corrected Kurt. "You could do it."

"I think I'd like a career kissing you," Kurt joked.

"Well, you'll never get anywhere without practice," Emma pointed out.

Kurt kissed her again, leaving her breathless. "God, I love you, Emma. I can't believe we're going to get to spend this whole tour together. I'm not going to let you out of my sight."

"It's a deal," Emma said softly, and kissed him again. But even as she was kissing him, a funny voice inside her was wondering: *He's not going to let me out of his sight? Now, is that a promise, or a threat?*

FOUR

"Yeah, I could definitely get used to this," Sam decided, propping her feet up on the dark green upholstered seat across from her. "No worries, cruising down the road in my tour bus, making all the boys weep because they can't have me . . ."

Just an hour earlier everyone had met at The Flirts' house to board the bus for their first show, which was that night in Boston. They'd practiced day and night for the past few days, and everyone was pumped for their first gig on the tour.

Carrie and Emma traded looks. "She's finally gone off the deep end," Carrie told Emma.

Emma nodded seriously. "Her very first moments on tour and she thinks she's Madonna."

"Madonna?" Sam scoffed. "Puh-leeze! That babe is seriously over the hill." She put her feet down and stared out the window. "Babe alert! Serious buff-dom in the red pickup truck to the east!" Sam waved to the two guys in the truck and blew them a kiss. "Heaven! I'm in heaven. . . ." Sam sang at the top of her lungs.

"Can't you shut her up?" Diana called from the front of the bus, where she was sitting with Sly.

"Hey, I sing for a living!" Sam objected. "People pay to hear these pipes!"

"Well, I'd pay to *not* hear them," Diana yelled back. "A dollar for every hour of your silence— that ought to be big bucks to someone like you."

"Remind me next time I get violently ill to hurl in her direction," Sam said in a low voice.

"Just picture her the way she looked when you threw your drink in her face at Carrie's party," Emma reminded Sam. "That ought to make you smile."

"It is one of my fondest memories," Sam replied. "Anybody hungry?" She reached over to the refrigerator and pulled out some dip, then took a bag of potato chips off the counter. "Tell me this isn't the coolest!" she added, ripping open the bag of chips.

"It is pretty terrific," Emma agreed with a smile. "I think I need to go kiss the driver," she added, and made her way up to the front of the bus to kiss Kurt.

"Ain't love grand?" Sam sighed, sticking some chips into the dip and popping them into her mouth.

"I think so," Carrie said, looking over to where Billy sat talking quietly with Pres.

"You're crazed for the guy, aren't you," Sam said, looking over at Billy.

"Yep," Carrie admitted. "I really am."

"So what did you decide about doing the Wild Thing?" Sam asked, reaching into the fridge again for a Coke.

"The Wild Thing?" Carrie repeated.

"Yeah, you know," Sam said, popping open her can of Coke. "The Horizontal Hula, the Bone-Jumping Jollies, the—"

"I get the idea," Carrie interrupted. "How about just calling it making love?"

"Well, I guess you could," Sam allowed dubiously. "But 'making love' sounds like a phrase from one of those yucky romance novels."

"I'll risk it," Carrie replied wryly. She took a diet Coke out of the fridge and popped the tab. "I've decided not to room with Billy," she said.

"No Bumping Uglies?" Sam asked innocently.

"Stop!" Carrie laughed. "I'm just not sure if I'm ready to . . . take that step with Billy, you know? And I don't want to feel pressured just because we're sharing a hotel room."

"Who's sharing a hotel room?" Emma asked as she walked back over to them.

"Not Carrie and Billy," Sam replied. She looked over at Emma. "How about you and Kurt?"

"Negative," Emma replied softly. "When the

53

time is right for me and Kurt we're going to be alone, not on tour with a bunch of other people."

"Gotcha," Sam nodded, downing the last of her Coke. "Well, this leads us back to the really big question—which one of us is going to room with the Wicked Witch of the West."

"Not me," Emma said. "It was bad enough being at the same boarding school with her all those years—I've already served above and beyond the call of duty."

"Well, it sure isn't gonna be me," Sam said adamantly. "I'll strangle the witch in her sleep."

Emma and Sam both looked at Carrie. "Don't look at me," Carrie said, holding her hands up at them.

"But you're the nicest," Sam said. "You're mature. You can ignore her."

"And you don't have to stand up there and sing with her either," Emma pointed out.

"Uh-uh!" Carrie protested. "No way! I told you, I'm moving a cot in with you guys."

"Why do that when I'll have that big queen-sized bed all to my lonely self?" Billy asked, coming up behind Carrie and nuzzling her neck.

She turned around and kissed him lightly. "Poor baby," she said with a laugh. "How about if I come visit you now and then?"

"I guess I'll have to settle for that," Billy said

with a shrug. "So did you guys decide on your sleeping arrangements?"

"The three of us are going to room together," Carrie told him.

"Bad idea," Billy said.

"Good idea," Sam corrected him. "If any of us have to room with Diana, Diana will be dead before morning."

Billy sat down next to Sam and pulled Carrie down onto his lap. "I'm serious—it's a bad idea. I know you guys aren't friends with Diana—"

"To put it mildly," Emma added.

"Yeah," Billy agreed. "But she's part of this band. It would be a really bad precedent if the very first time we went on the road there was one person no one would room with, you know?"

"So you room with her," Sam suggested.

"Thanks a lot," Carrie said, making a face at Sam.

"The way I figure it, this is only the first of a lot of tours for us, so we need to think long-term," Billy continued. "And I'm sure Carrie will always be traveling with us as our official photographer. . . ."

"My pleasure," Carrie said, leaning over to kiss Billy's cheek.

". . . so we've got four girls. We're paying for two rooms. You guys need to figure it out—two in one room, two in the other."

"Yuck," Sam said.

"Good luck," Billy said, lifting Carrie off his lap and getting up. "Let Kurt know what you decide—he's doing the room assignments. I'm off to go work on that new tune with Pres in the back."

"Well, I guess he told us 'employees' a thing or two," Sam said morosely.

"I suppose we should draw straws or something," Carrie said.

"We don't have any straws," Emma added glumly.

"Dental floss," Carrie suggested. She rummaged through her purse and got her dental floss, then she tore off three strings, one of which was much shorter than the other two. She rolled the three strings in her hands, leaving the top end of each sticking out of her fist. "Whoever draws the short floss gets Diana," she said.

Emma pulled out a string of dental floss, which turned out to be long. She smiled at her friends and waved the dental floss at them.

"Sam?" Carrie said. "It's either you or me."

Sam took a deep breath, closed her eyes and reached for a string of floss. She pulled. Out came a short string. "Damn!"

"Sorry," Carrie said. "Well, not really," she added.

"I knew I was going to lose! I just knew it!" Sam cried.

"What are you three up to?" Diana asked, getting some juice out of the fridge.

"Figuring out roommates," Emma said. "Did you have a preference?"

Diana narrowed her eyes and looked over at Pres and Billy. "Pres, I think," she decided.

"Hilarious," Sam said dryly. "Guess what. You're rooming with me."

"You?" Diana asked, looking as if she had a bad taste in her mouth.

"Believe me, I'm as overjoyed by the news as you are," Sam said.

"It's no big thing," Diana said with a shrug. "I don't plan to spend much time in my room, anyway, if you know what I mean." She shook her curls and made her way back to Sly.

"Nauseating," Sam commented.

"One of the lower life forms," Carrie agreed.

"Doesn't she worry about diseases?" Emma wondered.

Sam shook her head ruefully. "Me and Diana. Together. This is gonna be *some* tour!"

After they checked into their rooms at the downtown Boston Holiday Inn, Sam went right down the hall to Emma and Carrie's room. She didn't want to spend any more time alone with Diana than she absolutely had to.

"Howdy," Carrie said, opening the door when Sam knocked.

"Cool, it looks just like my room," Sam said, plopping down on Carrie's bed. "Except, of course, *she's* in there."

"Well, you can hang out in here whenever you want to," Emma assured her. She looked up at the tacky picture of a winter scene in New England that hung over the bed. The colors in the picture matched the faded shade of blue in the velour bedspread. *Okay, so it's not exactly the kind of first-class hotel you're used to,* Emma told herself. *You're here with your friends—that's what's important.* She lifted her T-shirts out of her suitcase and put them in the top drawer of the white laminated dresser.

"I don't know why you're bothering to un-pack. We're only staying here two nights," Sam reminded Emma.

"Habit," Emma said with a shrug, hanging a skirt in the small closet.

"Are you going to call your mother?" Carrie asked Emma, as she put her toiletries in the bathroom. Emma's mother, and the house where Emma grew up—when she wasn't off in Europe—were just across town.

"No," Emma said. "Frankly I'd just as soon she not know I'm in Boston."

"I guess I can't picture Kat Cresswell at a rock concert, at that," Sam agreed. "What time is it?"

"Almost four," Carrie told her. "Kurt said we

need to meet in the lobby at four-thirty to get over to the Gardens for the sound check."

"God, I have to get ready!" Sam yelped, jumping up from Carrie's bed.

"For a sound check?" Emma asked.

"You-know-who will probably be at the sound check," Sam said meaningfully. She sat back down on the bed and nervously bit a hangnail off her pinky.

Carrie and Emma knew very well just who Sam was referring to—Johnny Angel—one of the hottest young rock stars in the country. Last summer they'd all actually met Johnny Angel at one of his concerts—in fact, they'd gone to a party on a yacht with Johnny and various other musicians.

Johnny and Sam had really hit it off—in fact, Sam somehow convinced herself that Johnny Angel was It—the True Love of Her Life. She had gone into a private bedroom on the yacht with him, and just when things had gotten extremely steamy, his girlfriend came bursting into the room. His *girlfriend*! Sam had never felt so humiliated in her entire life.

Every time she thought back to that night, she wanted to die. She was certain she'd made a fool of herself in front of Johnny. At the time she'd been sure they shared something important, romantic, and real, only to find out that to

Johnny she had been nothing more than a pleasant diversion.

Sam winced just to think about how incredibly dumb she'd been about him. Johnny had been on her mind ever since The Flirts had won the tour with him (and boy, was that dumb luck or what?). Just a couple of nights earlier, in fact, she, Carrie, and Emma had stayed up until the wee hours hashing over just what Sam's approach with Johnny should be. Both Carrie and Emma had advised Sam to go slow, play it cool, and take a wait-and-see approach. And of course they had both reminded her what a great guy she already had.

"Tell me the truth, you guys," Sam said, "is he even going to remember me?"

"No one could forget you," Carrie said loyally.

"Thanks," Sam said, "but a zillion girls throw themselves at him every night. I'm probably just one of the masses."

"Well, if he doesn't appreciate how special you are, then he doesn't deserve you, anyway," Emma said, sitting down next to Sam.

"You guys are too much," Sam said with a smile. She looked down at the sweatpants and Mickey Mouse T-shirt she was wearing, and got up resolutely. "I'm definitely going to go change," she decided. "It'll give me more confidence."

"We'll meet you downstairs," Emma told her.

"Just remember," Carrie cautioned Sam, "don't try too hard."

"*Moi?*" Sam said. "I am the Queen of Cool. Later!"

"Testing . . . testing . . . one . . . two . . . three . . ." Billy said into his mike.

"Try it again!" the sound man called from the middle of the huge, empty house.

"Hey, check, paycheck," Billy said into his mike.

"Gotcha," the sound man said. "Okay, lemme hear from the girls."

"Testing . . . testing . . ." they each said in turn.

Sam kept looking around nervously. She'd changed into an old pair of jeans just baggy enough to settle around her hips, and a man's sleeveless T-shirt covered by her favorite thrift-store paisley vest. She'd put on lipstick, mascara, and her favorite perfume. But even though the sound and light guys were part of Johnny Angel's group, Johnny himself was nowhere in sight.

"Okay, got it," the sound man called. "Lemme hear your opening tune—what's it called?" The sound guy scanned the list Kurt had given him. "'Love Junkie'?"

"You got it," Billy replied. He nodded at Sly behind the drums, and Sly counted off. The opening strains of "Love Junkie" filled the Garden, the sound reverberating around the cavernous room.

"Hold it a sec," the sound man called, making some adjustment.

"Imagine this whole place full of people tonight," Emma said dreamily. "It doesn't seem real, does it?"

"I hope that lighting guy is planning to make the light hotter over here," Diana said, shaking her head petulantly. "No one is even going to see us!"

"Oh Diana, shut up," Sam said irritably, still looking around nervously for Johnny.

"What are you so tense about?" Diana asked Sam keenly. "And what do you keep looking around for?"

"None of your business," Sam snapped. The very last person in the world she planned to tell about her short-lived romance with Johnny Angel was Diana De Witt.

"Hey, can we get the babes down front for this dancing thing you've got marked in 'Wild Child'?" the lighting guy yelled from the back of the house. "I need to focus the spot."

"It's about time," Diana said huffily, and led the way to center stage.

"You want us to play some of it?" Billy called to the back of the room.

"Yeah, I need to see if I can pick 'em up in one spot or not," the lighting man replied.

"Okay guys, let's take it—'Wild Child,'" Billy said to the band.

Once again Sly counted them off, and Sam, Emma, and Diana went into their dance moves.

I hope Johnny sees me just like this, Sam thought, as she expertly executed her double pirouette.

"Cool! Got it!" the lighting guy called to the girls.

"Say cheese, babes!" a male voice called from just below the stage. The bright stage lights were blinding them, and they couldn't see who was down there.

"Who is that?" Sam asked, moving downstage and peering out into the house with her hand over her eyes.

"No! Not you, Big Red! Anyone but you!" the same voice yelled.

The lightman turned off the stage light at the exact instant that Sam recognized the voice. She felt a sinking feeling in the pit of her stomach.

It couldn't be. But it was.

Flash Hathaway.

The same guy who had promised to take modeling shots of her on the island, and then expected her to sleep with him in return. The same guy who had exhibited photographs of her in see-through lingerie—shots that he had promised were only for use in her private portfolio.

She loathed him.

"What the hell are you doing here, you rodent?" Sam demanded, staring down at the greasy photographer.

"Working, babe," Flash said irritably. "The Flash Man is *Rock On* magazine's photographer for the Johnny Angel tour. How the hell did a no-talent bimbette like you get hooked up with a band?"

Diana laughed. "Gee, I heard such horrible things about you, Flash, but I can see you and I are going to get along great!"

"We *have* a photographer," Emma said adamantly.

"Right," Carrie said, walking over to Flash. "Me."

"Ha," Flash barked. He fingered one of the many gold chains around his neck. "I know all about you, babe. You may have the booty, but you ain't got the shoot-y, if you catch my very basic drift."

Billy walked downstage and stared down at Flash. "Who the hell are you?"

"Flash Hathaway, *Rock On* magazine," Flash said. "My friends call me the Flash Man."

"Uh-huh," Billy said dubiously.

"I kid you not," Flash continued, "I can make you guys look like superstars in your shots."

"Cool," Billy said. "Well, we didn't know *Rock On* was sending a photographer. We brought our own."

"Strictly amateur city," Flash said confidentially. He brought the camera to his eye and snapped off a shot of Emma staring down at him incredulously. "Whoa, ice-princess, you still got that mine-doesn't-stink look—it's unbelievably sexy."

"Billy . . ." Carrie said, pleading for him to intervene.

"So, you'll both take pictures," Billy said with a shrug. "We all know what a great photographer you are," he added for Carrie's benefit.

"Oh great, just great," Carrie fumed, her hands on her hips.

"Hey, Big Red, I see you still haven't gone into the double-digits in the 'ta's' department," Flash yelled up to Sam as he aimed the camera at her.

"Die, you scum-sucking moron!" Sam shrieked down at him.

Something caught her attention from the side of the stage—and then Sam wanted to die herself.

Because Johnny Angel was standing there. And he had heard the whole thing.

FIVE

"Ladies and gentlemen, let's have a big Boston welcome for a very hot new band, Flirting With Danger!" the emcee's voice boomed through the Garden's sound system.

The crowd's applause was lukewarm, but the band was so intensely focused that they barely noticed. They jumped right into "Love Junkie," their adrenaline pumping them to new heights.

There're thousands and thousands of people out there! Emma thought to herself as she shimmied and swayed and sang her backup vocal parts. *This is just unbelievable!*

Sam caught Emma's eyes as they did a spin and she winked. Sam felt fabulous, and she only hoped that Johnny Angel was watching her now. Maybe it would make up for the embarrassing scene that afternoon. Of course, Sam hadn't stood around long enough to know if Johnny had recognized her or not. She'd run off the stage in the other direction and gone out to the bus. Fortunately the sound check was over, and soon everyone joined her. Johnny's dressing room was on the other side of the labyrinthine backstage area, and Sam hadn't seen him at all since they'd arrived for the first gig of the tour.

Love Junkie.
Love Junkie, baby!

Billy sang the final line in a raspy wail, Sly hit his final drum combination and the tune finished. The applause was warmer now—the audience might have come to see Johnny Angel, but they were already beginning to enjoy his opening act.

"Thank you very much," Billy said into the mike. Behind him Jay began to play the lyrical keyboard line that opened "You Take My Breath Away." The lights changed, and Billy sang soulfully.

Each and every day
You take my breath away. . . .

Sam turned sideways, as did Emma and Diana, and they went into the simple swaying movements they used on this ballad. Sam was facing stage right, where she saw, to her annoyance, Flash Hathaway snapping pictures of them.

And then she saw *him*. Standing right next to Flash was Johnny Angel. He was dressed in a black muscle T-shirt and baggy jeans. His blond hair was slicked back off his gorgeous, chiseled face and his muscular arms gleamed in the lone offstage light. A diamond stud glinted in his ear. Johnny folded his arms, leaned on one hip, and looked right at Sam.

And then he winked.

At least Sam thought he winked. *Maybe he didn't. Maybe I just wished it,* Sam thought to herself.

In unison, on the next verse, the girls turned back to the front, continuing their swaying movement. Now Sam couldn't see Johnny without turning her head to the side, so as much as she wanted to check him out, she couldn't.

What more can I say
You take my breath . . . away.

Billy finished the last hushed note, and the crowd burst into enthusiastic applause. Now Sam snuck a quick look to her right, and there he was! Johnny Angel! He was still looking at her! And he was applauding!

Diana looked over to the right and saw him,

then she turned to Sam. "Now that is one hot guy," she said thoatily.

"Yeah," Sam agreed, trying not to stare at Johnny.

"He's been checking me out ever since we came on stage," Diana said smugly. "I can't wait to get my hands inside those baggy jeans of his."

Sly began the drum riff for a new tune Jay Bailey had written, "Ride the Wave." Sam automatically began to sway and sing "ride, ride, ride" on the backup parts.

Was Johnny really looking at Diana and not me? Sam wondered. *Maybe he doesn't remember me at all!*

The next tune was "Wild Child" and Sam tried to put Johnny out of her mind as she executed the complicated dance moves. Still, in the back of her mind was: *I hope he's watching me now.* Sam danced full-out, being as wild as she could possibly be, just in case.

After a few more songs, the set was over, and the band left the stage to applause, cheers, and whistles. Some people even held up lighters to show their approval.

"Wow, that was so much fun!" Emma cried when they got offstage. Kurt was standing there and she jumped into his arms exuberantly.

"Hey, I like this greeting!" Kurt said, wrapping his arms around her.

"I gotta tell you, that went really well," Billy said to them. "It can be very tough to be the opening act—a lot of times the crowd won't even listen."

"But they loved us," Diana said, lifting some curls off her sweaty forehead.

"Let's go back to the dressing room," Billy told Kurt. "I want to go over a few notes."

"Bye, gorgeous," Kurt whispered to Emma before he left.

"We were extremely hot out there," Diana said.

"It went pretty well," Pres agreed in his understated style, his arm around Sam's waist.

"Pretty well," Sam teased him. She tickled his chin with some of her hair. "Honestly, you are the most laid-back person on the face of the earth."

"Not always," Pres said, nuzzling her neck. "Come on back to my dressing room with me and I'll see if I can whip up some excitement for you, little lady."

"Oh, I . . . uh . . . thought I'd stand here and watch Johnny Angel's show," Sam said. Emma shot her a look. "He's really good," she added quickly.

"*Rock On* magazine says he's the male version of Madonna," Diana said, peering across the stage to where she'd seen Johnny before.

Pres shrugged. "Not my style," he drawled. "Catch ya later then." He walked back to the dressing room area.

Sam watched him leave and then grabbed Emma and pulled her close. "I saw him!" she hissed.

"Johnny?" Emma asked.

"During our set. He was over there." She pointed to the other side of the stage. "I think maybe he winked at me."

"Just be really careful about Pres, okay?" Emma whispered.

"I'm not doing anything!" Sam protested.

"Well, good," Emma replied. "I'm going to take a shower." She walked away.

Diana leaned against a wall and crossed her arms.

Great, Sam thought glumly. *She's going to wait and watch him, too. Just what I need is competition from Diana De Witt.*

"Ladies and gentlemen," the emcee announced. "*Rock On* magazine is proud to present Polimar recording artist . . . Johnny Angel!"

The crowd went wild. Strobe lights bounced crazily around the stage. And a giant ice-cube-like object with smoke billowing out of it descended from the rafters. Slowly the cube broke apart, and inside, amidst the clouds of smoke, was Johnny Angel. He stood there a moment, bathed in a pulsing red light, then he stepped down and walked onto the stage.

"Johnny! Johnny! I love you!" girls were shrieking from the crowd.

Johnny stood completely still. Then he spun around quickly three times and went into a wild gymnastic dance as his band cooked behind him.

He's unbelievable, Sam thought. *He's come so far since he was opening for Graham Perry a year ago.*

Sam stood there mesmerized while Johnny did an hour and a half of singing, dancing, and rapping for the crowd of about ten thousand people. He had a band of five guys, and six backup singer/dancers—four guys and two women. It was an incredible show, and the cheering audience demanded three encores before they let him end his set. Sam found herself applauding and screaming right along with the masses. She got so excited she even turned to say something to Diana, only to find that somewhere along the way Diana had left.

"I love you!" Johnny rasped into the mike, picking up some of the flowers and panties that had been thrown to him. Then he ran off the stage.

Right toward Sam!

Johnny Angel stopped right in front of Sam, his muscular arms full of the flowers and sexy lingerie. Sweat was pouring off him. He smiled at Sam.

"Pick one," he said easily.

"Wh . . . what?" Sam stammered.

"A gift," Johnny said with a laugh. He opened his arms and handed Sam the flowers and lingerie.

"Thanks, I'll settle for the flowers," Sam said, finding her voice. She loosened her arms and let three pairs of flimsy panties fall to the floor.

Johnny laughed out loud. "I know you," he told Sam.

Omigod, Omigod, he actually remembers me! Sam realized. "Oh, do you?" she said, very coolly.

Johnny cocked his head to one side. "Yeah. You're the girl who yelled at that photographer guy this afternoon. That was great!"

Sam's heart fell. So, he didn't remember her after all. She had been alone with him, had kissed him for hours. She had even believed they had a future together, and he didn't even remember her. "On second thought, I'm allergic," Sam said flatly, thrusting the flowers back at Johnny. She turned on her heel and headed toward her dressing room.

"Hey! Where are you going?" Johnny called after her.

She just kept walking.

"So, what happened?" Emma asked when Sam got to the dressing room. Emma had used the shower in the bathroom connected to their dressing room. She looked clean and refreshed in white jeans and a white cotton shirt.

"Don't ask," Sam said glumly, falling into a chair. Suddenly she felt how grubby she was, still sweaty and dirty from the show. "Yuck. I need a shower."

"Everyone else is already on the bus in the parking lot," Emma said.

"They waited for me?" Sam asked, throwing her stuff into a large canvas bag.

"Sly wanted to check out Johnny's drummer, and Diana wanted to check out Johnny's anatomy, so you weren't the only one," Emma assured her. "And Carrie was out there taking pictures through Johnny's set, too."

"Hey, I've just been invited to a party," Diana said, swinging into the room.

"Whose?" Sam asked, gathering up the last of her cosmetics.

"Johnny's," Diana replied, lifting her fringed minidress over her head.

"Johnny Angel?" Sam asked.

"Yep," Diana replied. "I just had the most *luscious* conversation with him. He said you guys can come, too, if you want. The whole band can come, I suppose. Do I have time for a shower?"

"No, everyone else is waiting for us on the bus," Emma told her.

"How did you happen to have a conversation with him?" Sam asked Diana, her eyes narrowed.

"I waited for him in his dressing room, silly," Diana said. "There are certain advantages to having these backstage passes, you know." She lifted a sweatshirt over her head and stepped into a pair of perfectly faded jeans.

"I'm sure he thinks you're just another groupie," Emma told Diana haughtily. "Not that such a thing would bother you, of course," she added.

"Emma, believe me, I stand out from the crowd," Diana assured her, throwing her canvas tote bag over her shoulder.

"What party did he invite us to?" Sam asked her.

"He invited *me*," Diana corrected her, "but like I said, it's cool if anyone else in the band comes, too. It's in his suite in an hour."

"I didn't even know they had suites at the Holiday Inn," Sam murmured.

Diana gave her a pained look. "Honestly, get the hay out of your teeth. Johnny Angel is hardly staying at the Holiday Inn. He's got the entire top floor of Boston Bay Towers Hotel."

"I knew that," Sam murmured, turning red.

Diana shook her head. "Catch you on the bus," she called and hurried out the door.

"So Johnny really *was* winking at her," Sam said morosely. "I can't believe I actually thought he'd remember me."

"Well, it's his loss," Emma said righteously. She looked around to make sure she hadn't forgotten anything. "You ready to go?"

"Yeah," Sam said with a sigh.

"Cheer up," Emma said, as they turned out the light and left the dressing room. "I have a feeling Diana and Johnny Angel have a case of dueling massive egos. They probably deserve each other!"

An hour later Sam knocked on Emma and Carrie's door. She'd taken a shower and changed into jeans and a T-shirt while Diana debated what to wear to Johnny Angel's party. Sam told her she wasn't interested in going, and Diana was hardly going to try to talk her into it. Sly was planning to go to talk with Johnny's drummer, and Jay was going because he was always up for a party. Pres had invited Sam out for a bite to eat, but she was too depressed to want to be with him.

"Come on in," Emma said, opening the door to their room.

"I didn't even think you guys would be here,"

Sam said, plopping down on Carrie's bed. "I figured you'd be with your guys—I just took a chance."

"Billy, Pres, and Kurt went out to eat," Emma said.

"Billy said he'd call me as soon as he got back," Carrie told Sam.

"And I suppose you're going to do something with Kurt," Sam said glumly to Emma.

"Maybe we'll go down to the lounge and have a drink or something," Emma said. "Why don't you and Pres come?"

"I'm too depressed," Sam said. She pulled a pillow over her face. "How could I have ever believed that he'd remember me?"

Carrie pulled the pillow off Sam's face. "What is the big deal, would you mind telling me that? So what if some self-absorbed rock star doesn't remember you?"

"I think Pres is hotter than Johnny, anyway," Emma added, opening a bottle of clear nail polish.

"This doesn't have anything to do with Pres." Sam pouted.

"Well, you're acting like a baby," Carrie said firmly. "Snap out of it."

"Yes, Mom," Sam said with a small laugh.

"Well, I'm sorry, but this is just not a big deal," Carrie said. "Why let Johnny Angel ruin this incredible experience?"

"You're right," Sam agreed. "I know you're right."

"Good," Emma said.

"Still, maybe if I went to his party and made a big play for him—in the most understated way, of course . . ." Sam mused.

Carrie picked up a pillow and heaved it at Sam. "You're hopeless!" she yelled.

"Pillow fight!" Sam yelled. She scrambled to her knees and bopped Carrie with the other pillow. Carrie threw a pillow at Emma.

"My nails are wet!" Emma cried, but she gave in and picked up the pillow to bash Carrie.

The girls were jumping all over the beds, screaming with laughter, and bopping each other with pillows when they heard a pounding on the door.

"I'll get it!" Carrie yelled gaily. She jumped off the bed and went to the door. Kurt and Billy were standing outside.

"I thought there was some kind of battle going on in here," Billy said, giving Carrie a kiss.

"Pillow fight," Carrie said happily, still breathless.

"I love pillow fights," Kurt said with a grin. He strode across the room and quickly picked up Emma in a fireman's carry, slinging her over one shoulder. She shrieked as he dropped her on the bed, pummeling her with both pillows.

"Stop! Stop!" she yelled, laughing so hard she could barely catch her breath.

"Say 'Kurt is the greatest guy on the planet,'" Kurt told her, still pummeling her with the pillows.

"Kurt is the greatest guy on the planet!" Emma yelled between fits of laughter.

"Such a compliant girl," Kurt said, and dropped the pillows.

"I'll get you back later," Emma promised him.

"Let's go," Billy urged Carrie quietly.

"Where?" she asked.

"My room," he said in a low voice.

"What about Pres?" Carrie asked.

"He's hanging out in Jay's room at the moment, reworking the chorus of 'Ride the Wave.'"

"All work and no play!" Emma called out gaily.

"I agree," Billy told Carrie quietly. "Let's go play."

Carrie just looked at him.

"No pressure," he promised her. "I just want to be with you."

"And I want to be with you," she admitted. She reached for his hand and pulled him up. "Let's go."

Kurt looked over at Sam. "Uh, Sly's in my room right now, sleeping."

"I thought Sly and Jay were both going to Johnny Angel's party," Sam said.

"They are, eventually," Kurt replied. "According to Jay, it'll go on all night."

"It's no big deal," Billy added. "Johnny's drummer told me Johnny has a party every night when he's on the road."

"What a fun guy," Sam intoned.

"I thought you were always up for a party," Kurt told Sam.

"Not in the mood," Sam said sourly. Kurt kept staring at her. "Oh, you want me to leave so you can be alone with Emma!" she blurted out, the light finally dawning.

"Oh no," Emma said quickly. "You don't have to leave. . . ."

"Hey, it's cool," Sam said, getting off the bed. "I'm sure my lovely roomie has left for the party, so I'll just go . . . order everything on the room service menu, or something. See ya!"

Sam went down the hall to her own room, fitted the key card in the door and went in. Then she stopped in her tracks. Diana had left the room a total mess. A dozen outfits were strewn over the floor. Powder trailed from the bathroom to the bed. A lipstick had been ground into the carpet. Three different pairs of shoes were on the dresser.

"What a pig!" Sam cried indignantly. *I might be messy but I do not trash hotel rooms,* she thought as she angrily picked up the pink lipstick and threw it in the garbage. She sat down on her bed and sighed heavily. *Here I am, my first night on the road, and I'm wasting it being depressed. I really do have to snap out of this!* Sam told herself firmly. *I know. I'll call Pres in Jay's room. When he's done we can go do something or other.*

But just as Sam was about to pick up the phone to dial Jay's room, it rang, startling her.

"Hello?" Sam answered.

"I knew it was you," came a deep male voice.

"Pardon me?"

"I knew it was you," the voice repeated. "This is Johnny."

Sam's heart hammered in her chest. She clutched the phone receiver tightly in her hand. "Johnny who?" Sam said insolently.

Johnny laughed. "Yeah, that's absolutely the girl I remember. Last year? The party on the yacht in Miami? I was just teasing you back-stage tonight, but you never gave me a chance to tell you."

"I was busy," Sam said flippantly. *Stay cool, Sam,* she warned herself. *Don't let him know how much this means to you.*

He laughed again. "So, tell me, why aren't you at my party?"

"I think Diana's enough for any guy to han-dle," Sam said pointedly.

"I told her to invite you," Johnny said. "Did you get the message?"

81

"Yeah," Sam lied. *I can't believe he told Diana to invite me and she acted like it was an afterthought. On second thought, I can believe it!*

"So?" Johnny asked.

"So, have fun with Diana," Sam said, as if she couldn't care less.

"She's cute," Johnny allowed, "but not my type."

"Oh, what's your type?" Sam asked.

"You," Johnny said softly. "I never forgot about you, you know."

"Hmmmm," Sam said noncommittally.

"I really want to see you," he added.

"Where are you?" Sam asked. "I don't hear a party."

"I'm in one of the bedrooms," Johnny said. "The party is out in the living room—at least for the moment."

"Oh," Sam said, then winced at her reply. *Oh? Scintillating. You have to do better than that, babe!* "I mean, sounds like it's barely gotten started," Sam added.

"It's just a party like lots of others," Johnny said. "So, I was thinking, how about if I bring the limo over there and pick you up?"

Sam gulped hard. "That might be okay," she said casually.

"Great," Johnny said. "I'll be there in like fifteen minutes. Meet you downstairs?"

"Sure," Sam agreed, "okay," as if rock stars picked her up in their limousines every day.

"Cool," Johnny said softly. "See you in a few."

Sam hung up and sat there, unable to move. *Did that really just happen?* she asked herself. Then she screamed. "Holy-Moley and Good Golly Miss Molly! I'm going out with Johnny Angel!" She raced around the room, changing into a camisole but leaving on her jeans. She pulled on her trademark red cowboy boots, sprayed herself with perfume, redid her red lipstick, and threw on her black leather motor-cycle jacket with the painting of Minnie Mouse on the back. Then she scrutinized herself in the mirror. "Sam, babe, you are too hot to live!" She blew a kiss at her reflection and headed out the door.

A long black limo pulled up right on time, and Sam bopped out to the car while a uniformed driver held the door for her.

Look at me, world! Sam felt like yelling. But she didn't. She got in the car and sat next to Johnny as if she did this kind of thing every day.

She never noticed Pres, who was just coming out of the cocktail lounge off the lobby. But he saw her. He watched Sam get into the limo, and then he watched it pull away. And he saw the license plate, too. It read J-ANGEL.

SIX

"So then I told him, 'If you come in your limo, I might go with you,'" Sam confided, reaching for a blueberry muffin.

"You didn't," Emma said.

"I did," Sam chortled happily.

It was late the next morning, and the three girls were sitting together in the dining room of the Holiday Inn. Sam had already told them about how Johnny Angel had called her the night before. Now she was telling them the rest of the details about the previous night.

"Unbelievable," Carrie said. "So he really did remember you after all!"

"Yeah," Sam agreed blissfully.

"So what happened then?" Carrie begged, pouring herself some more coffee.

"Well . . ." Sam began slowly, a wicked gleam in her eye. "The answer to that is really personal. . . ."

"You mean he . . . you . . . ?" Emma ventured.

"You *slept* with him?" Carrie shrieked.

"Fooled ya!" Sam crowed. "Actually, he showed up in his limo, picked me up, and we spent most of the night riding around Boston in the lap of luxury! Mega-romantic!"

"He didn't put the moves on you?" Carrie asked.

"I didn't say that," Sam answered, smiling. She finished the last of her muffin and reached into the basket for a croissant.

"So what happened?" Emma asked, sipping her tea.

Sam shrugged. "I just told him I wasn't ready for that—and then I kissed him again."

"He was okay with it?" Carrie asked, astonished. She knew that Johnny Angel had a reputation as a stud, and probably wasn't used to being turned down.

"Okay with it?" Sam asked rhetorically, nibbling on a piece of bacon. "Well, maybe he wasn't thrilled," she allowed. "But no way was I about to act like one of his bimbo groupies—"

"The name Diana springs to mind," Emma murmured.

Sam laughed. "What he told me is, 'Sam, good things are worth waiting for.'"

"Johnny Angel said that?" Carrie questioned dubiously.

"I always told you he was more than just a pretty face. And bod," Sam added.

"But last year on the yacht you two practically did it, and then his girlfriend came in!" Emma reminded Sam.

"His ex-girlfriend," Sam said, defending Johnny. "Besides, I was the one who acted like a fool. He never promised me we were having some big love affair. That's just what I wanted to believe!"

"And now you're older and so much more mature," Emma said.

"As a matter-of-fact, yes," Sam said smugly. "Anyway, you didn't hear the rest of the story."

"So he dropped you off after driving you around Boston all night?" Emma prompted her.

"Wrong. *He* didn't drive me around Boston. His *limo driver* drove us around Boston," Sam corrected her. "Then, the *limo driver* dropped me off."

"What about the party?" Emma asked, taking a sip of tea.

"What party?" Sam asked innocently.

"The party in his suite," Carrie reminded her.

"Oh! That party!" Sam exclaimed. "The one Johnny left just so he could be with me." She took a long drink of her fresh-squeezed orange juice. "Well, you'll have to ask Diana about that. She was there. I wasn't."

As if on cue, Diana De Witt appeared in the

doorway of the Holiday Inn restaurant. She was wearing baggy white cotton pants tightly belted, and a white cotton bra top that showed off her perfectly aerobicized abdomen. First she looked at the girls' table—no way was she going to sit there voluntarily. Then she glanced around the room—every other table was taken. Finally, with a sigh loud enough for them to hear, Diana ambled her way over to Sam, Emma, and Carrie and sat down.

"Diana," Sam greeted her sarcastically, "long time no see."

"No kidding," Diana said coldly. "Did you and Johnny He's-No-Angel take a room together last night or what? He told everyone he was leaving to pick *you* up."

Sam grinned triumphantly. "You'll have to ask Johnny," she said coyly. "That is, if he'll speak to you. Frankly, I doubt that he'd waste his time."

"Oh, spare me," Diana snorted. "You think you're such hot sh—"

"Not think, Diana," Sam interrupted regally. "Know. I didn't see you spending the night with him. By the way, how was the party that he wasn't at?"

"The tour's not over yet," Diana shot back. "And I think that between Johnny and Pres, I'll end up taking my pick. Anyway, I'd rather get room service than sit here with you lowlifes."

With that, she got up from the table and strode away.

"Not a happy camper," Carrie observed wryly, taking a bite of toast.

"God, it is *so* much fun to get the better of her for a change!" Sam exclaimed.

Emma looked at Sam curiously. "Why did you deliberately give her the impression that you slept with Johnny Angel when it's not true?"

"Because she wants him so badly that it's driving her nuts," Sam replied blithely. "That's a good enough reason for me."

"Don't you think something like that could, well . . . backfire?" Carrie asked Sam slowly.

"Backfire how?" Sam asked.

"What if Diana tells Pres and Pres believes her and—"

Sam cut Carrie off with a wave of her hand. "Never happen," she said. "Pres'd know that Diana was only trying to get him jealous."

"You're pretty confident," Emma observed.

"That's me!" Sam joked.

"Well, that's the you you *pretend* to be," Emma said softly. "We know you better."

"Yeah," Sam said with a malicious grin. "But Diana doesn't."

"What if Pres found out some other way?" Carrie asked her, a troubled look on her face. "Wouldn't you feel bad?"

"Hey, since I didn't really sleep with Johnny,

there isn't very much to find out, is there?" Sam explained.

"I think there is," Emma said. "I think Pres would feel badly that you were hanging out with Johnny all night."

"Pres is a big flirt," Sam pointed out with irritation. "Besides, he and I don't have any kind of exclusive agreement or anything."

"Still—" Carrie began.

"Look, Pres isn't gonna find out," Sam shot back, crushing another piece of bacon in her mouth. "Anyway, Johnny Angel's a big star!"

"What does that have to do with it?" Emma asked her with exasperation.

"Everything," Sam said seriously. "Just everything. Anyway, I know what I'm doing."

"I hope so," Emma said. "I'd hate to see you mess it up with Pres."

"Hey," Sam said, trying to change the subject. "I almost forgot—where did you spend last night, Carrie?"

Carrie smiled. "I cannot tell a lie," she said. "I spent it in Billy's room."

"Whoa girlfriend! Get down!" Sam yelled.

"Not so fast," Carrie said. "Nothing happened."

"Nothing happened?" Sam demanded. "You spent the night in his room and nothing happened?"

89

"That's right," Carrie said, taking another sip of coffee.

"Yeah, sure!" Sam snorted. "And a bear does not use the woods for his litter box."

"Sam!" Carrie laughed. "I could say the same thing about you and Johnny Angel."

"The difference is," Sam pointed out, "in my case I would be telling the truth."

"Well, me too, Miss Know-It-All!" Carrie said. "We slept in the same bed, and things actually got pretty far, but . . ."

"But what? But what?" Sam prompted her. "The story is just getting juicy!"

"But we . . . stopped," Carrie finished.

"Why?" Emma asked her.

"Good question," Carrie responded. "I've been thinking about that myself."

"You weren't ready," Emma suggested.

"Hey, she's no virgin," Sam reminded Emma. They both knew that Carrie had lost her virginity during her senior year of high school to her former boyfriend Josh, with whom she'd had a five-year relationship.

"Being a virgin doesn't have anything to do with it!" Carrie said with irritation. "You think that just because I slept with Josh it makes it any easier for me to decide to sleep with Billy?"

"Yes," Sam said flatly.

"Well, it doesn't," Carrie told her.

"But doesn't it seem silly sometimes," Emma ventured. "I mean, where is the line drawn, you know?"

"It does," Carrie agreed with a sigh. "As far as we went, maybe we should have made love."

"Well, why didn't you?" Sam nudged her with her elbow as she spoke.

"I don't know!" Carrie cried. "On one hand I think I'm ready to take that step with Billy, but on the other hand it just wasn't the right time and place," Carrie explained. "Which is what I told Billy."

"So what did he say?" Emma asked.

"He said he felt frustrated," Carrie admitted. "But he's hanging in there."

"What's with all these really cool guys?" Sam joked. "I thought all men are scum."

"Sometimes they are," Emma muttered.

"What?" Sam asked. "Did I just hear Miss Manners make a disparaging remark?"

"It's Kurt," she sighed. "Last night wasn't the greatest, that I'll admit."

"Don't tell me . . . *you're* the one who ended up doing it!" Sam guessed.

"Not funny," Emma replied quietly.

"Sorry," Sam apologized.

"Kurt and I had a fight," Emma explained.

"Again?" Sam asked.

"We don't fight that much," Emma retorted, then she sighed. "Yes, we do. Lately we do. It's just that sometimes he loves me so much that I feel . . . suffocated! And then I feel guilty for feeling that way!"

"What happened last night?" Carrie asked Emma.

"Oh, nothing special," Emma recounted. "After you guys left, we just stayed in the room and talked and talked."

"So?" Sam asked. "Sounds totally harmless."

"It was," Emma said, "until it was time for him to leave. I was beat!"

"What did he do?" Carrie asked her.

"He wouldn't leave," Emma admitted. "He kept telling me how much he loved me, and how he wanted to spend the night with me—God, it was like someone trying to put a plastic bag over my head! Finally, I just told him to get out!"

"He left?" Carrie asked.

"He left extremely ticked off," Emma clarified. "At me."

"Don't you love him anymore?" Sam asked. "I always think of you two as the perfect couple!"

"I do love him," Emma assured her friend. "I just . . . I don't know! I really don't!" she said with frustration.

"Maybe . . ." Carrie ventured. "Well, could this have anything to do with what happened with Adam?"

Earlier in the summer, Emma and Carrie

had gone with Sam to visit her birth mother in California (Sam was adopted), and Emma had fallen hard for Sam's older brother, Adam. Even though Adam wanted to continue the relationship—he wanted to come to Sunset Island and visit her—Emma had vowed it was over, and she'd never told Kurt about what happened.

"Maybe," Emma murmured. "Maybe I still feel guilty about that."

"Maybe that's because you took Sam's advice and didn't tell Kurt about it," Carrie said, shooting a look at Sam.

"It was good advice!" Sam cried.

"No, it wasn't," Carrie said.

"I think it's even more than the thing with Adam," Emma continued. "Sometimes Kurt loves me so much that I . . . I just want to run away! I think he wants to keep me like a dog on a leash! If only he realized I'm not going anywhere!"

"So much for the cool guy department," Sam joked.

"Can't you talk to him?" Carrie suggested reasonably.

"Talking to him," Emma said, draining the tea in her cup, "doesn't seem to do any good." She blinked tears out of her eyes.

"Hey, lighten up!" Sam finally said. "We're three incredibly hot babes on a rock and roll tour!"

"Speaking of the tour," Carrie looked at her

watch, "our bus leaves for Philly in a half hour."

She stood up from the table, and Emma and Sam joined her. Together, they made their way out of the restaurant and into the main hotel lobby. At the far side of the lobby, there was some kind of commotion. They walked over to see what it was.

"Yeah, babe! You got the look! You're killin' me, babe!" said a familiar voice, from the center of a big circle of people.

"It's Flash!" Carrie groaned. "No one else sounds quite like him."

"I wonder what he's doing here?" Emma mused.

The girls pushed their way to the center of the knot of people. What they saw was astonishing.

It was Diana, wearing a fake fur coat with a red lace teddy under it, draped across the lobby's couch. Flash Hathaway was dashing this way and that, snapping photograph after photograph. The crowd ooohed and aaahed as Diana struck one sexy pose after another. And Kurt stood near Flash, watching the whole scene with interest.

Every time Flash stopped for a minute, Diana made some flirtatious comment to Kurt, who clearly seemed to be enjoying himself. When he noticed Emma staring at him, his face hardened. At one point Diana pranced over to him and he put his arm around her waist and whispered something in her ear. Diana giggled and danced back to the couch.

"I can't believe what I'm seeing," Emma said.

"It's just photos for the tour," Carrie said, trying to rationalize what was going on and make Emma feel better.

"In the Holiday Inn lobby?" Sam snorted. "With De Witt in her underwear? Please!"

"I'm leaving," Emma announced, and turned to go back to her room.

"I'll come with you," Carrie said, and they hurried to the elevators.

Sam strode over to Kurt. "What the hell do you think you're doing?"

"Flash is taking some shots for the tour," Kurt said, his face turning red.

"Oh, give me a break, Ackerman," Sam snapped.

"Hey Big Red, get out of the way," Flash said. "Can't you see there's art happening here?"

"What's the matter, Sam?" Diana cooed. "Jealous? Or is it your frigid friend Emma who's jealous? I see she left."

"Me, jealous of you?" Sam said to Diana. "Of you? That's a joke."

"Then it's Emma who must be jealous," Diana concluded, posing seductively on the couch. "How sweet!"

"You call this being a good road manager?" Sam barked at Kurt.

"You don't need to tell me how to do my job, Sam," Kurt said in a steely voice. "And these shots are going to be in the paper in Philly, for your information. It's good publicity."

"Let me give you some advice, Kurt," Sam said in a low and furious voice. "If I were you, I would get my butt upstairs real fast and apologize to Emma." Sam turned and strode away without waiting to see if Kurt was taking her advice.

Johnny Angel's limousine picks me up again. There are rose petals spread over all the cushions inside. Johnny's waiting for me there. He's wearing a black muscle shirt and tight ripped blue jeans. I climb in. He kisses me on the lips, then tells his driver to take us on a tour of Philly. Near Independence Hall, he pulls the curtains on the limo so no one can see in, and he puts up the partition between us and the driver. Then—

"Hey, Sam," Pres said conversationally, sliding onto the tour bus couch beside her. Sam snapped guiltily out of her daydream.

"Hey, yourself," Sam replied, making room on the couch. She stared out the window and saw a big "Welcome to New Jersey" sign. "We just crossed the New Jersey state line. How much farther?"

"About two hours," Pres answered, looking out the window at the stores that lined both sides of Route 17.

"Cool," Sam said easily. "I'm really up for this gig."

"Sam," Pres said quietly, "where were you last night? I came lookin' for you late—thought we might could get a soda."

Sam thought quickly. *If I tell him about Johnny Angel, he'll be really pissed. So I'll lie. What he doesn't know won't hurt him. And if Diana's already said something to him, he wouldn't have been asking me where I was.*

"Uh," Sam said, "what time was that?"

"Around eleven-fifteen," Pres said.

"I was . . . jogging," Sam invented.

"Where?"

"There's a treadmill in the gym on the second floor," Sam made up quickly. *After all,* she thought to herself, *if it's not true he can't go back and check.*

"Hmm," Pres said. "It's funny, because I saw someone who looked a lot like you gettin' into a limo with the license tag J-ANGEL. That wouldn't have been you, would it?"

"Ah, yeah!" Sam said, smiling brightly. "That was after I ran."

"After," Pres echoed.

"Yeah, there was a message from Johnny for me at the front desk when I got back," Sam improvised as she went along. "We're old friends."

"You met him before?"

"In Florida with Emma and Carrie," Sam told the truth this time.

"Oh," Pres drawled noncommittally. "Well, don't you go desertin' your old friends jus' 'cause you're renewin' some acquaintances."

"I won't!" Sam said brightly.

Dodged a bullet right there, she thought to herself. *I think he believes me.*

"Well," Pres said easily, "I gotta go check something with Kurt. Excuse me."

"He and Emma had a fight," Sam said confidentially, taking a glance at the unchanging scenery.

"Oh," Pres said. "So that explains it."

"Explains what?"

"Explains that Kurt's about as pleasant to be around today as a one-legged man in a butt-kickin' contest," Pres muttered.

"I love those quaint expressions!" Sam laughed. Then she reached over and pulled him toward her, and kissed him on the lips.

"What was that for?" Pres asked.

"You said don't desert your old friends," Sam said. "I'm not."

Pres gave Sam a lazy grin before he went to the back of the bus.

Sam smiled to herself and stared out the window. *Like I've always said,* she reminded herself, *two guys for every girl is the Sam Bridges motto.* She sighed happily, propped her cowboy boots up on the seat opposite her, and went back to her delicious Johnny Angel daydream.

"Sam?"

Sam sighed and opened her eyes. It was Kurt.

"Can I talk to you a minute?"

Sam shrugged. "It's a free country."

Kurt sat down next to Sam and stared down at his hands. "Look, about that thing with Diana—"

"Excuse me, but aren't you talking to the wrong person about this?" Sam interrupted. "Shouldn't you be talking to Emma?"

"She won't talk to me," Kurt said.

"Did you try?" Sam asked.

Kurt ignored the question and looked past Sam out the window as if he were trying to find some answers. "Have you ever been in love? I mean really in love?"

"I don't know," Sam answered honestly. "Probably not."

"Then you don't know how I feel," Kurt said earnestly. "I'd do anything for Emma—"

99

"Then why do you pull this stupid stuff with Diana?" Sam queried.

"Well, Emma just ticks me off sometimes—"

"Oh, good answer," Sam replied sarcastically. "*So* mature."

Kurt sighed. "Look, I never said I was perfect—"

"Good," Sam interrupted. She looked over her shoulder at Emma sitting by herself, staring forlornly out the window. "Do you know how much you hurt her with that dumb little display in the hotel lobby?"

"They really *were* publicity pictures," Kurt muttered.

Sam gave him a look of disgust.

"I guess I was kind of hoping maybe you could talk to Emma for me," Kurt said sheepishly.

"Well, I can't," Sam said bluntly. She saw the hurt on Kurt's face. "Look, you guys have to work this out yourself," she continued in a kinder voice. "But I'm telling you, you can't love someone by suffocating them."

"Is that what she thinks?" Kurt asked, again looking hurt.

"Ask her," Sam suggested. "But maybe if you just weren't so . . . intense with her, everything would work out."

Kurt stood up in the aisle. "Thanks, I'll keep that in mind," he told Sam. He gave her a crooked smile. "Sometimes love stinks, you

100

know?" Then he walked to the back of the bus.

Sam looked out the window. *Wow,* she thought to herself. *Amazing. I ought to charge by the hour—Samantha Bridges: Advice to the Lovelorn.* She closed her eyes and leaned her head back against the seat. *Now, where was I?* she thought dreamily. *Ah, yes, Johnny Angel was pressing his hot lips against mine. . . .*

SEVEN

"Thanks, Philly, you've been great!" Billy yelled over the cheers of the crowd, and the band ran offstage.

"More! More!" the crowd cheered. Billy looked at Pres, who had just as huge a grin on his face as Billy did. They'd just finished their second show of the tour at the Philadelphia Spectrum, and the audience wanted an encore.

"What should we do?" Emma asked over the noise.

Billy scratched the day's growth of stubble on his chin. "I say the public is always right—let's go get 'em!"

"'Born to Run'?" Pres asked, naming a classic Bruce Springsteen song they'd worked on.

"You got it!" Billy agreed. "Let's do it!"

The band ran back onto the stage, the girls taking their positions in the back behind their mikes. Billy picked up his guitar and the crowd cheered wildly. He went right into the opening riff of "Born to Run." The whole audience knew the song, and people sang along on the chorus. When the number finished the whole place went crazy with enthusiasm and The Flirts ran off the stage again.

"Wow, that was even better than Boston!" Diana cried when they got offstage.

"This is so much fun, I'm amazed it's legal!" Sam added with a laugh.

"Great show, guys," Kurt said, standing in the wings with a clipboard under his arm. The guys in the band high-fived him as they went by on their way back to their dressing room. Kurt looked closely at Diana's white fringed dress. "These costumes need cleaning," he told her. "Wear one of your other outfits for the next gig—I'll see that those get to the dry cleaners."

Diana sidled up to Kurt and put one finger on his lips. "Want to help me out of it like you did the other day?"

Before Kurt could answer, Emma stormed past them and headed for the dressing room.

"You did that on purpose," Kurt told Diana crossly. "I only helped you out of it because Flash was taking those shots."

"But you loved it, didn't you," Diana purred maliciously.

"Go scratch your claws somewhere else," Sam told her, grabbing a towel from Kurt to wipe her face.

"Meow," Diana replied, and sauntered off toward the dressing room.

"Bitch," Sam said. She looked around. "Where's Carrie?"

"Taking pictures from the house, I guess," Kurt told her, his eyes on the checklist on his clipboard. "Don't forget to get your dress to me before you get on the bus."

"Hey, cutie," a low voice called to Sam. She turned around and found Johnny Angel smiling at her.

God, he's gorgeous, she thought to herself. *Any girl in America would want to be me right now.*

"Hi," Sam said.

He looked her over carefully. "Love the way you shake that fringe."

Sam did a small shimmy. "You're kind of poetry in motion, yourself," she told him insouciantly. Inside, she didn't feel nearly as cool as she sounded. *Please let him like me,* she prayed. *Please let it be special this time.*

He took a step closer and put his hands around Sam's waist. "So . . . what are you doing later, pretty lady?"

"Why? You having another party you don't want to go to?" Sam asked flirtatiously. She wrapped her arms around his neck.

"I thought maybe we'd have our own party," Johnny replied, leaning over to lick her lips.

"Well, maybe," Sam began feigning noncha-lance, "but—"

"Hey, Kurt, you got the ace bandage? Sly turned his ankle," Pres was saying as he walked toward them. He took in Johnny Angel with his arms around Sam's waist, then he turned back to Kurt.

"Yeah, it's in the first-aid kit in the bus," Kurt told him. "I'll go get it."

"No man, I'll get it," Pres said. "Suddenly I feel like some fresh air." He turned and walked abruptly away.

"Damn," Sam cursed softly, dropping her arms from Johnny's neck.

"My competition?" Johnny asked. He made it clear from the tone of his voice that he didn't feel he had any real competition.

"Hey, I'm a free woman," Sam said lightly.

"That's what I like to hear," Johnny said, kissing Sam softly. "Meet me in my dressing room after the show, okay?"

"You got it," Sam agreed.

"Hey, kiss for luck," he said, holding her close again. This time he kissed her passionately, and Sam kissed him back until she felt weak-kneed and breathless.

"Great suck-face shot, Big Red!" an all-too-familiar voice cheered.

"Flash," Sam fumed, turning to him. "Get the hell away from me!"

"Gimme that film," Johnny said, taking a menacing step toward Flash.

"Sure, no problem!" Flash said without hesitation. "Didn't know you'd object, my man."

"You want to take my picture, you ask," Johnny said in a steely voice.

"Ladies and gentlemen, *Rock On* magazine presents Polimar recording artist . . . Johnny Angel!" boomed the announcer's voice.

"You get that film to my road manager," Johnny said to Flash, pointing a menacing finger at him. "I'll be checking."

"No prob, my man," Flash assured him.

"Gotta go," Johnny said, kissing Sam quickly. "Later."

"Amazes me that a big star like him would want to jump your bones, Big Red," Flash said, popping some gum in his mouth. "I guess there's no accounting for taste, huh?"

"You are the mental niblet of the Earth," Sam told him.

"Nah, babe, you are," Flash said.

The crowd noises increased as Johnny Angel's band began their opening riffs.

"Did it ever occur to you why Mr. Tall, Blond, and Famous doesn't want me taking his pic with his tongue down your skinny throat?" Flash continued, yelling over the noise from the stage.

"Because you're an intrusive worm who isn't

good enough to lick between his toes?" Sam suggested.

"Kinky," Flash mused. "You try it already?"

"God, I can't believe I'm standing here sparring with you," Sam said with disgust. "Just leave me alone." She pushed past him and headed for her dressing room.

Flash chuckled and aimed his camera at the stage. "Yeah," he said out loud to himself, clicking off a few shots as Johnny stepped forward out of his ice cube and walked through the smoke. "Johnny Angel's got the gold, and Big Red's gonna get the shaft."

It was a couple of hours later. On the bus back to the hotel Emma hadn't said one word to Kurt, and he hadn't spoken to her either.

Why does it have to be like this? Emma thought despondently. As soon as they got back to the hotel, Carrie went off somewhere with Billy. Sam hadn't even gotten on the bus, but had been whisked away from the Spectrum in Johnny Angel's limo—a fact not lost on Pres. Emma took a shower, put on some jeans and a denim shirt and went down to the lobby to buy every single fashion magazine in the gift shop.

I won't even think about Kurt, she vowed, and paid for the eight magazines.

"Hi there," Pres said, ambling into the gift shop. He looked over Emma's pile of magazines.

"Looks like you're in for some serious reading."

"I think it's don't-think-about-Kurt reading," Emma confessed.

"Well, I could probably use some don't-think-about-Sam reading, myself," Pres said ruefully. His eyes met Emma's. She smiled and he laughed. "Dang, if we aren't two sorry fools."

"I guess we are, at that," Emma said with a sad smile.

"Listen, how about if we skip the reading material and go get a drink," Pres said spontaneously.

"Oh, thanks anyway," Emma said, "but I'd be terrible company."

"Now, I doubt that," Pres said. "How about food, then. Did you eat before the show?"

Emma shook her head no. "I'm always too nervous to eat before we go on."

"Well, we've got that in common," Pres said. "How about if we go get us some supper?"

"Oh, I don't know. . . ." Emma began.

"Shoot, girl," Pres said, "even a bitty thing like you has gotta eat."

Emma laughed. "Every now and then."

"Well then?" Pres asked.

Emma thought about it a second. "Why not?" she finally said. "It beats reading alone in my room."

"Now you're talking," Pres said. "One of Johnny's roadies told me there's a great barbecue place near here that's open all night. You game?"

"Sure," Emma said with a shrug. She looked down at her magazines. "I'll just take these upstairs first."

"I have a feelin' once you get up there you'll get to feelin' sorry for yourself and never come back down," Pres said. He picked up the pile of magazines and handed them to the surprised-looking girl behind the counter. "Can y'all hold these 'til the morning?"

"Sure," the girl said. "I'll put them behind the counter."

"Thanks," Emma said.

Pres held the door for her. "Let's go!"

"God, that was great," Emma said, daintily licking some barbecue sauce off her little finger. "I can't believe I ate that entire plate of ribs!"

It was an hour later, and Emma and Pres had both ordered the rib plate special at Hot Mary's Rib Shack. Emma, who rarely ate red meat much less greasy ribs, had eaten ravenously.

"Watch out," Pres said in a teasing voice. "You down enough of this stuff you start talkin' with a southern accent!"

Emma smiled at him. Pres was such good company, so easy to be with. *Unlike Kurt,* she added in her mind, then instantly felt guilty at having such a disloyal thought.

"That boy thinks you hung the moon, you know," Pres said, obviously referring to Kurt. It was as if he were reading her thoughts.

"He's a great guy," Emma said, taking a sip of her water. "But . . ."

"Yeah, it's those 'buts' get you into trouble," Pres replied.

"I love him, Pres. I really do," Emma said earnestly. "But it's like he's so afraid he's going to lose me that he . . . he won't let me breathe!"

"I've known girls like that," Pres said, nodding. "It always ended up making me move further away instead of closer."

"Exactly!" Emma exclaimed. "And also . . . well, maybe I feel guilty about something that happened in California that I never told Kurt about," Emma said in a low voice.

Pres raised his eyebrows and didn't say a word.

And Emma found herself blurting out the whole story about Sam's brother, Adam, and how she had never admitted to Kurt that for a while she'd fallen for another guy.

"I know it was terrible of me—" Emma began.

"I don't think so," Pres said. "Loving Kurt doesn't mean you're ready to get married or even to get all that heavy," Pres said with a shrug.

Emma looked at him curiously. "Well, now

110

that I've bared my heart to you, what's going on with you and Sam?"

"That's the same question I've been asking myself," Pres admitted. "That girl plays too many games."

"Can I get you anything else?" the waitress asked, clearing away their dirty dishes.

"No, thank you," Emma said.

"Coffee?" Pres asked.

"Well, if you're having coffee I'll have tea," Emma said.

The waitress nodded and hurried off.

"You were saying?" Emma prompted Pres.

"It's like this," Pres said. "I really care for Sam, but these little games of hers are gettin' real tired."

"Sam is . . . afraid to be in love, I think," Emma said slowly.

"Maybe so," Pres acknowledged. "I don't want to tie her down—hell, I don't want to tie myself down! But I want some honesty and some grown-up behavior."

"Me too!" Emma exclaimed. "I wish Kurt was more like you!" Emma clapped her hand over her mouth, and blushed a bright red. "I didn't mean that the way it sounded. . . ."

"Hey, it's okay," Pres assured her, reaching easily across the table to put his hand over hers. "Sometimes I wish Sam was more like you."

I love the way his hand feels, Emma thought to

111

herself. *What would it be like to kiss him?* Pres rubbed his fingers over the back of Emma's hand, and a little thrill traveled down her spine. *This is terrible!* she told herself. *I can't be having these feelings about my best friend's boyfriend!*

"Well!" she said a little too brightly, quickly pulling her hand away. "I guess we should be going. . . ."

"We just ordered coffee and tea," Pres reminded her.

"Oh, right," Emma agreed, obviously flustered.

"Relax," Pres said with a lazy grin. "I wasn't hitting on you, if that's what you're thinking."

"Oh, no, I didn't think that," Emma said hastily.

"Good," Pres said.

The waitress put Pres's coffee and Emma's tea on the table.

Emma changed the subject to safer ground—music. She and Pres talked easily about the band.

But in her mind, Emma felt terrible. Because she knew the truth. *I did too think Pres was hitting on me. And the very worst part of it was . . . I liked it.*

"God, Carrie, you feel so good," Billy groaned, running his hands down Carrie's back.

"So do you," she whispered, smiling in the dark.

They were in Billy's hotel room, lying on his bed. Though she had all her clothes on, Carrie could still feel the heat of Billy's body practically scorching her through her thin T-shirt. Somewhere in the back of her mind she wondered where Pres was, but anyway the door was latched, so he wouldn't even be able to get in with his key. Carrie gave herself up to the incredible sensations of being in Billy's arms.

He kissed her again, his mouth searching hers, then he kissed her neck, his mouth traveling downward. "You're so beautiful," Billy said. Gently he lifted the bottom of her T-shirt, a questioning look in his eyes.

Carrie reached down and lifted her T-shirt over her head. Then she stood up and unzipped her jeans, and let them fall to the carpet. Now she wore just a lace teddy over her bra and panties. Billy was bare-chested, wearing only a pair of gym shorts. He pulled Carrie back down on the bed and kissed her passionately.

"I really want to make love to you, Car," he said in a low voice.

"Me too," she admitted.

"Good," Billy said, reaching around to unhook her bra underneath her teddy.

"Billy, wait!" Carrie said, catching his hand in hers.

"What?"

"Well, I didn't plan . . ." Carrie began. "I mean, I don't have any . . ."

"Birth control?" Billy asked. "That's okay, I'll be careful."

Carrie moved slightly away from Billy. "Billy, that's dumb. You're just saying that because you want to do it—"

"Of course I want to do it," Billy said, running his fingers down her arm. "I'm in love with you. You're in love with me. We've been together a long time, and we're not little kids. This is what grown-ups do when they're in love."

"I know," Carrie said. "But I'm not going to do something stupid."

"How can our making love be stupid?" Billy asked, with a hint of irritation in his voice.

"Look Billy, for one thing, I don't know who you've slept with," Carrie said, feeling embarrassed.

"No one in a really, really long time," Billy assured her, leaning on one elbow.

"Well, for me there's only been Josh," Carrie said, naming her high school boyfriend. "And that was a long time ago too."

"So, then—?" Billy asked, reaching for her again.

"So then we still need to have safe sex," Carrie said. "Have you ever been tested for AIDS?"

Billy's hand stopped caressing her arm. "You're kidding me."

"No, I'm not," Carrie said in a low voice.

"I don't screw around, Carrie," Billy said. "You already know that."

"I *do* know that," Carrie said earnestly. "But what about your last girlfriend, from right before you met me?"

"Bonnie?" Billy asked.

"Right," Carrie said. "Didn't you tell me she was kind of wild, that she'd had lots of boy-friends?"

"So?"

Carrie sat up. "So I think maybe you should have a test for HIV before we become lovers," Carrie said, biting her lower lip. *Wow. I can't believe I just said that,* she marveled. *I didn't even know I felt that way until just this minute! That's a big part of what's been holding me back!*

Billy sat up slowly, hurt clouding his eyes. "Don't you trust me, Car?"

"It's not you, Billy!" Carrie cried. "I trust you and I love you. But this disease kills people, even really nice trustworthy people!"

"So . . . you're telling me that even if we go out and buy rubbers and have safe sex," Billy said slowly, "you won't make love with me unless I get tested for HIV?"

"Right," Carrie said in a small voice.

Billy ran his hand through his hair. "I can't believe you're doing this to us."

"Billy," Carrie said earnestly. "When we make love, it's like we're having sex with everybody that your ex-girlfriend ever had sex with, don't you see?"

Billy shook his head. He got up slowly, grabbed his jeans from the chair, and stepped into them. "I . . . I don't know what to think, Carrie," he said gravely.

"Please don't be mad!" Carrie cried anxiously. "Please try to see my point of view!"

"I guess I'll have to think about it," Billy said. "Alone," he added pointedly.

Carrie got up and quickly put her T-shirt and jeans back on. She felt like crying, or like begging Billy to understand, to not stop loving her, but she wouldn't let herself do that. "I hope you see my point of view," Carrie said quietly, her hand on the doorknob. "I really do love you, Billy."

"That's pretty hard for me to believe right now," Billy answered.

Carrie gave him a sad smile, and walked out the door.

I won't cry, Carrie told herself as she unlocked the door to her own room. *There's nothing to cry about. Billy loves me, and once he thinks about this he's going to agree with me.*

Emma was already sound asleep, so Carrie

undressed and got ready for bed as quietly as possible. But once she lay down she found she couldn't sleep. She glanced at her watch and was surprised to find it was already three o'clock in the morning. *I feel awful,* she realized. *Anxious. Scared. Afraid Billy won't understand. Afraid I'll lose him. Oh, please God, don't let me lose Billy!*

Impetuously she got up out of bed and grabbed the hotel pad and pen that was on the dresser, then she tiptoed into the bathroom so she wouldn't wake Emma.

Maybe if I write down how I feel, Carrie thought to herself, *it will help me sort it all out.*

No one knows love, especially me, she found herself writing. She stared at that line, and then, as if by magic, a melody line wended its way into her mind. She sang the line in her head: *No one knows love, especially me.*

Carrie spent the next two hours writing out everything that was in her heart. She started out writing to help herself sort out all the feelings she was having about Billy, but the amazing, incredible thing that happened was . . . she ended up writing a song.

EIGHT

Carrie let the water from her morning shower cascade down her body, and she turned her face up to the jets. *Did I really write a song last night?* she asked herself.

She'd woken up wanting to talk the whole thing over with Emma, but Emma was already gone. Carrie read over the lyrics which she'd left on the nightstand the night before. Was it possible that her song was . . . good?

Hey, Carrie, you are no writer, she'd reminded herself. *And on top of that, you aren't very musical and you certainly can't sing. So just forget the whole thing.* And yet, as she shampooed her hair the melody and the words kept drifting through her mind.

No one knows love the way that I do.
No one knows how to play it so cool.
So who can I trust? Where should I be?
No one knows love, especially me.

No one could hurt me the way that you do.
You say that you love me, and I play the fool.
So why am I crying? And why can't you see
That no one knows love, especially me?
No, no one knows love, especially me.

"Hi," Emma said, when Carrie came into the room towel-drying her hair.

"Oh hi. You're back," Carrie said.

"I woke up early and went to work out," Emma said, pulling off her sweaty white leotard. "What was that you were singing in the shower?"

"Oh, nothing," Carrie said, embarrassed that Emma had heard her singing.

"I didn't even know you could sing," Emma said, heading for the shower.

"I can't," Carrie called to her.

"Well, it sure sounded like you could to me," Emma called back as she turned on the shower.

While Emma showered, Carrie read over her song again. Knowing that Emma wouldn't be able to hear her over the rushing water, she sat on her bed and sang it out loud. As Emma turned off the shower she was singing the very last line, but she stopped mid-phrase.

"I heard you!" Emma called out to Carrie. She came into the bedroom wrapped in her black velvet robe with the white lace collar. "You really *do* sing!"

119

"No, I don't," Carrie protested. She reached into a drawer and pulled out a Yale sweatshirt and some jeans.

"It's such a pretty melody," Emma said. "Where did you hear it?"

"Um, the radio, I guess," Carrie lied.

Emma went to the closet and pulled out a black and white cotton minidress, and slipped it over her head. "Who sang it?" Emma asked.

"Oh, I don't remember. . . ." Carrie's voice trailed off.

Okay, I'm not in the habit of lying to Emma, and I'm not going to start now, no matter how embarrassed I get that she heard me singing.

"Em, I lied," Carrie said, chagrined. "The truth is . . . I sort of wrote it, myself. Last night," she added.

"You did?" Emma asked, clearly surprised.

"Yup," Carrie said. "I guess I should stick to taking pictures, huh?"

"Are you kidding?" Emma pressed her. "I think it's really good. Seriously."

"Come on, you don't have to say that," Carrie mumbled.

"I'm not, I mean it!" Emma replied. "You wrote the melody *and* the lyrics?"

"Mmmm," Carrie said noncommittally.

"Sing the whole thing for me," Emma urged her.

"No way," Carrie said quickly.

120

"Why not?" Emma asked her. "I don't bite."

"Because . . . because I feel like an idiot!" Carrie admitted.

"Carrie, this is me you're talking to," Emma said.

"Okay, you're right," Carrie agreed reluctantly. "If you can't risk looking like a fool in front of your best friend, where can you risk it?"

"That's the spirit," Emma said with a laugh. "But I'm telling you, your song is good."

"Don't tell anyone I'm doing this," Carrie begged.

"I won't," Emma assured her.

"You've got to promise," Carrie qualified.

"I promise," Emma repeated.

"Swear on Katie Hewitt's life!" Carrie joked.

"I swear," said Emma.

"Okay, here goes," Carrie said. She took a deep breath and closed her eyes. It was too scary to sing it and watch Emma staring at her at the same time. When she finished singing she opened her eyes slowly to see Emma's reaction.

"You think it's okay?" Carrie ventured.

"Okay?" Emma repeated. "I think it's great! You are so talented, Carrie!"

"I'm not. . . ." Carrie protested.

"You are!" Emma insisted. "We should do it on the tour!"

"Oh no," Carrie said hastily. "I'm strictly amateur."

"I loved it," Emma said matter-of-factly.

"I don't love it," Carrie admitted. "It needs . . . I don't know. Something more."

"A bridge, maybe?" Emma ventured.

"What's that?" Carrie asked.

"Well, the way you have the song structured the hook comes at the end of each verse," Emma explained.

"The part that goes 'No one knows love, especially me'?" Carrie asked.

"Right," Emma said. "What comes before that is the verse. So if you wanted to add a bridge, it would be a third melody that hooks from verse to verse or from verse to hook. And usually it's a lyric that adds something to what you've already said."

Carrie shook her head. "How do you know so much about songwriting?"

"Well, I've learned all these songs that Billy and Pres wrote and it seemed really interesting," Emma said. "So I went out and bought a book about it."

"Huh," Carrie marveled. "I never knew it was such a . . . planned thing!"

"It is," Emma assured her. "Your bridge might be something about how you're afraid of losing this person and you're also afraid of showing how scared you feel."

"Uh-huh," Carrie said, her brow furrowed with thought. "How about . . . like . . . 'so if I trust you, show you my heart, will it be the end . . . '?"

"Or only the start!" Emma finished the line quickly.

"Good, good, I like that!" Carrie exclaimed. She reached for her song lyrics and wrote in the bridge, then showed it to Emma.

"Great, and then you go back to the first verse, and then repeat the chorus line twice," Emma said, pointing out those places to Carrie.

Carrie closed her eyes. "I need a melody for the bridge." She thought a moment. "Something like . . . la-la-la . . ." and she sang a simple melody that she thought might work.

"Terrific!" Emma encouraged Carrie. "Now, sing the whole thing again from the top. See if it works."

"Sing it with me," Carrie begged. "I won't feel like nearly as much of a fool."

"Well, I'll try," Emma said. "I don't know the whole thing." Emma moved over to Carrie's bed so she could see the lyrics, and the two of them sang Carrie's song.

"Carrie, it's so fabulous. I mean it!" Emma cried, hugging Carrie exuberantly. "Wait until Billy hears this!"

"No!" Carrie yelled. "Absolutely not! I had a

fight with him last night, which is why I wrote this in the first place!"

"A bad fight?" Emma asked.

"I don't know," Carrie sighed. "I told him I want him to get an AIDS test before we sleep together."

Emma thought about that a minute. "Do you really think people like us need to worry about that?"

"Yes, I really do!" Carrie exclaimed.

"But we're not intravenous drug users, and we're not bisexual, so . . ." Emma shrugged.

"So how do I know who Billy's last girlfriend slept with?" Carrie asked. "I don't!"

"You're right," Emma finally said. "You're absolutely right. So what did he say?"

"He said he needed to think about it." Carrie sighed. "Don't you think if he really loves me he'd want to make absolutely certain that I'm safe?"

"I do," Emma agreed.

"So, I guess you can see why I'm not singing this song for him," Carrie said.

"No," Emma disagreed. "I think you should sing it for him, anyway. Maybe it'll even help him understand."

"I am not singing it for Billy, Emma," Carrie said, getting up to brush her hair in front of the mirror. "I'm no singer."

"You are too," Emma insisted.

"No, I'm not. Look," Carrie said finally, "it's bad enough that you want Billy to hear it. So why don't you sing it?"

"Because it's your song," Emma said, slipping some black ballet flats onto her feet.

"That's okay," Carrie said. "You sing it to him. Then at least it'll sound good."

"You sure?" Emma asked her.

"Never surer in my life," Carrie responded, standing up.

"Well, okay," Emma said with a shrug. "Let's go."

Emma was incredibly nervous, but she sang the entire song to Billy in her high, clear soprano, and then looked at him expectantly. Carrie sat in the one cushioned chair in Billy and Pres's room, staring at the floor. She was afraid to look at Billy to see his reaction.

"Carrie?" Billy called softly.

"Yes?" Carrie slowly looked up and over at Billy.

"You are a girl of many talents," Billy said. "And one of them is definitely songwriting."

"You think it's okay?" Carrie ventured.

At least I'm not embarrassed if he thinks it's at least okay—maybe a five on a scale of ten. At least I won't be totally mortified.

"No," Billy said, "I don't think it's okay."

Carrie's face sank.

"I think it's great."

"What?" Carrie said, stunned.

Billy smiled a wide and brilliant smile. "I said I think it's great and I think the rest of the band needs to hear it right now."

"You're kidding," Carrie said.

"Nope," he assured her. "Just watch me."

He picked up the telephone and called the health club on the second floor, where he knew that Pres, Jay, Diana, and Sly were all hanging out in the sauna. He had a brief conversation with Pres on the phone, and within ten minutes the rest of the band was all piled on the floor of his room.

"Where's Kurt?" Jay asked.

"Out running errands," Billy said. "Where's Sam?"

"Don't know," Carrie said.

"You know?" Billy asked Pres. Pres shook his head no.

"Maybe you ought to ask Johnny Angel," Diana smirked.

Billy ignored her. "This is band business. If she misses a meeting, it's her problem."

"So what's this big meeting about?" Sly asked. "I didn't even get to shower yet."

"Emma's got a song someone gave her that she wants us to hear," Billy said.

"And that's why we needed a big emergency meeting?" Sly asked.

Billy's jaw moved angrily. "Sometimes I don't

126

get you, Sly. I mean, what are your priorities, man? I'd really like to know."

"Forget it," Sly mumbled. "Sorry."

Billy nodded once, tersely. "Okay. Now I've heard this tune, and I really like it. I want to know what the rest of you think. Emma?"

"I'm so nervous," she confessed, pushing her hair behind her ears. "Singing for you guys in this hotel room is much worse than singing on stage!"

"You'll be great," Pres said kindly, giving Emma a wink.

"Yeah," she agreed nervously. She took a deep breath and started to sing. She had to refer to Carrie's lyric sheet and when she got to the new bridge she faltered for just a moment but got the melody back quickly, and by the time she came to the end, she sang it out in her lovely soprano.

No one knows love, especially me.
No, no one knows love, especially . . . me.

When she finished, there was dead silence in the room.

"Wow," Pres finally said, "that gave me chill bumps so big you could ski down 'em."

"Great tune," Sly remarked.

"Ditto," Jay chimed in.

All around the room, heads were nodding up and down.

"What's it called?" Pres asked.

Billy smiled. "You'll have to ask the writer. Carrie?"

"*Carrie* wrote that?" Diana exclaimed.

"No, a small farm animal wrote it, Diana," Emma said sweetly.

"Well, I'd believe that before I'd believe it was her," Diana muttered.

"It's called 'No One Knows Love,'" Carrie said in a small voice.

"That'll work," Jay said nodding. "I can just hear the piano part underneath the finish." His fingers played a silent riff on his jeans. "Yeah!"

"So," Billy said, "do we add it to the show?"

Sly shrugged. "It's a killer tune, why not?"

"You up to singing it?" Jay asked Billy.

"Well . . ." Billy began.

"Wait a second. Excuse me," Carrie interrupted. "I'm really, really glad that you like my song, but I don't think a guy should sing it."

Billy stared at her. "Well, at the risk of pointing out the obvious, we have a guy lead singer in this band."

Yeah, and it's that guy lead singer who made me upset enough to write the song in the first place! Carrie thought to herself. But she didn't say that. Instead she said, "I know. But there's no rule that a girl can't sing lead on one tune."

128

No one said a word. Everyone looked at Billy.

"What are you saying, Carrie," Billy asked, "that I should give up singing lead?"

"Just on this song," Carrie said. "It's from a woman's point of view, and I think a woman should sing it."

"Gimme a break," Diana said, rolling her eyes. "You aren't even in the band!"

"And I'm not going to sing it," Carrie assured her. "Emma is."

"Me?" Emma squeaked.

"Emma is a backup!" Diana protested.

"But she sang the hell out of that song," Pres said, giving Emma a grin.

"Just to show you I'm willing to be fair about this," Billy said, "we'll vote on it."

"Do the backups get equal vote?" Diana asked.

"Yeah, this one time you guys can vote, too," Billy said. "I don't want anyone to think my ego is too big to be cool about this." He shot Carrie a nasty look. "Who's in favor of our rehearsing this number and adding it to the show with Emma singing lead by, say, Washington, D.C.?" Billy asked. "That'd give us three days to work on it. All in favor?"

Pres raised his hand immediately, then Jay and Sly raised theirs, and finally Billy did, too.

"I suppose I should vote for myself," Emma said nervously, raising her hand.

Everyone looked at Diana. "Forget it!" she fumed. "At least we should audition the number and see which backup sings it the best. And since Sam can't sing and I sing better than Grace Kelly over there, everyone knows it'd be me!"

"Sorry, Diana, you are out-voted," Billy said. "We'll start working on it tomorrow afternoon."

Billy stood at the door as everyone except Carrie left his room. She sat in a large chair in total disbelief.

This cannot actually be happening to me, she thought. *I'm going to have a song I wrote sort of as a joke performed in front of a zillion people? What if they hate it?*

"You really have talent, Car," Billy said, sounding stiff.

"Thanks," Carrie said. "And thanks for being big enough to let Emma sing lead on it."

Billy shrugged. "I'm cool."

They sat in silence for a moment. Finally, Carrie got up. "Well, I guess I'll be going. . . ."

"Wait a sec," Billy said, jumping up. He put his hands on her shoulders. "About last night. I shouldn't have acted the way I did. It was just . . . really sudden."

"You mean you'll take the test?" Carrie asked, her eyes lighting up.

"I mean I'll think about what you said," Billy said. "That's all I'm saying for now."

"Well, it's better than nothing," Carrie repeated softly.

"And I really don't want to let this come between us," Billy continued. "You know what I mean?"

"I do!" Carrie cried, throwing her arms around him. "I love you so much."

"Right back at ya, Carrie," Billy said with a smile, and then he kissed her.

Sam's jaw nearly bounced off her late lunch of spaghetti when Carrie told her excitedly that Emma was going to get to do the solo of Carrie's new song, "No One Knows Love."

Sam had shown up back at the hotel around two o'clock, and she had immediately collared Carrie to come into the restaurant with her, claiming she was dying of starvation.

"Time out, time out," Sam said, actually putting down her fork. "You're telling me that you wrote a song, and Emma is going to get to sing lead on it, and this all happened between last night and today?"

"Yeah," Carrie said, taking a sip of her diet Coke.

"But . . . but why Emma?" Sam sputtered.

"Well, she's a really good singer, and I didn't think a guy should sing my song, and the band voted on it," Carrie explained.

"But it should be me!" Sam cried, outraged at the injustice of it.

"You?" Carrie asked her matter-of-factly.

"Yes, me!" Sam said. "I'm the one with the big future in show business. Emma doesn't even care about it!"

"She cared enough to be at the meeting this morning," Carrie reminded Sam.

"Well," Sam said, "how the hell was I supposed to know there was going to be a band meeting? Besides, we backups are 'employees,' remember? We don't get to vote, anyway!"

"This time Billy let everyone vote," Carrie told her. "Except you weren't there to cast your ballot."

"I had other plans," Sam mumbled.

"Billy was kind of irritated," Carrie reported.

"He should plan better," Sam retorted. "Whoever heard of a band meeting at eleven-thirty A.M.?"

"I didn't realize being in the band was a regular-hours job," Carrie said, feeling a little irritated that Sam was taking such a bad attitude about the whole thing.

"I was busy," Sam said quickly.

"You were with Johnny Angel again, right?"

"Well, what if I was?" Sam retorted defensively.

Carrie shook her head with disgust.

"It's different this time, Carrie," Sam said

earnestly. "I was such a child a year ago; I let him walk all over me. . . ."

"And now everything's different?" Carrie asked dubiously.

"It really is!" Sam assured her. "I mean, last year I was just some kid he met at a party, but this year I'm in the band that's on tour with him; it's a whole different thing!"

"I don't know, Sam. . . ." Carrie began.

"And I'm not sleeping with him, either," Sam added quickly. "And he knows I'm not going to! So don't you think that proves there's more to this than just him wanting to get into my pants?"

"I hope so," Carrie said. "I just think you've got to keep your priorities straight."

"Meaning?" Sam asked, still mad that the band had given the big solo number to Emma instead of to her.

"Meaning that you're a part of The Flirts, not a part of Johnny Angel's band," Carrie said.

"I know that," Sam said. She swallowed a piece of bread. "Is . . . is everyone mad at me?"

"Well, I think you should start showing your face more often, if you don't want them to *get* mad at you," Carrie explained.

"What about Pres?" Sam asked, biting her lower lip.

"I think if you don't quit screwing around, you could lose him," Carrie said bluntly.

"I'll be careful," Sam promised.

"It's not a matter of being careful, Sam," Carrie tried to explain. "It's . . . oh, just forget it."

"I don't want to hurt Pres," Sam said. "But I can't stop seeing Johnny. I just can't."

"Well, then, maybe you should talk to Pres about it, instead of just avoiding him," Carrie suggested.

"Yeah," Sam agreed, staring at what was left of her spaghetti. "It's just really hard for me to do that."

"But try," Carrie urged her.

"I will," Sam promised.

"Anyway," Carrie said, trying to lighten the mood, "if you're not around, I can't take photos of you that will make you rich and famous."

"Now you're talking," Sam said, smiling at her friend gratefully.

"Really, Sam," Carrie advised. "We all love you, and we love Pres, too. We don't want to see either one of you get hurt. So keep your eye on the ball."

"I will," Sam promised. But even as she was saying those words, she was picturing herself stretched out in the back of a limousine, sipping champagne, in Johnny Angel's muscular arms.

NINE

"I can't go through with this," Emma told Carrie.

It was three nights later, the night that Emma would sing lead on "No One Knows Love" in front of thousands of people in Washington, D.C. They were backstage in the dressing room at the Malcolm X Theater Center. Emma and Sam were putting the finishing touches on their makeup, and Carrie had just come backstage to wish Emma luck on her solo.

"Of course you can," Carrie told Emma. "You've been rehearsing the song for three days with the band. You're going to be terrific."

Emma turned around to look at Carrie, her hands shaking visibly. "What did I get myself into?" she whispered.

"Look, you know I would tell you if you were anything less than wonderful, right?" Carrie asked Emma.

"Maybe," Emma replied in a quavering voice.

135

"Of course I would," Carrie said firmly. "And believe me, you sing my song better than anyone else ever could."

"But . . . I'm so scared!" Emma exclaimed. "I've never been so scared in my life!"

Carrie turned to Sam, who was attaching a pair of false eyelashes to her eyelids. "Sam, come on. Help me!" Carrie urged.

Sam held her fingers over her left eye while the glue dried. "You sing the song okay, Emma," Sam said reluctantly. "However, I still think I should be singing it and not you."

"Sam!" Carrie objected.

"Well, I'm just telling the truth," Sam replied hotly. "Look at her! She's a nervous wreck! She doesn't even want to do it. Do you think this makes any sense?"

"She's nervous because she's never done it before," Carrie said, "not because she isn't terrific! I read that Laurence Olivier used to barf every night before he went out on stage, and he was the greatest actor of all time!"

"If it means this much to you, maybe we should ask Billy if you can sing it," Emma said to Sam. She looked completely miserable.

"Maybe we should," Sam agreed.

She stood up and reached for the man's oversized suit jacket, circa 1940s, that went over her black bra-top. On the bottom she wore men's oversized baggy pants cinched tightly with a belt at the waist. Both the jacket and the pants were studded with rhinestones. The girls had found the suits in a used clothing store, and Kurt hired a seamstress to hem them and add the studs. For certain numbers they would also wear rhinestone-studded men's fedoras on their heads.

"Ignore her," Carrie told Emma. She shot Sam an angry look but Sam deliberately didn't meet Carrie's eye.

"This is ridiculous," Emma cried. "We're fighting over something stupid! I don't care about singing the song!"

Diana came swinging through the dressing room door as Emma was speaking. "Glad to hear you don't care about singing the song," Diana said, "because frankly with your thin, little voice no one in the audience is even going to listen." She reached for her fedora on the top of the clothes rack. "Obviously I should be singing it."

"I hate this!" Emma wailed, burying her head in her hands.

Carrie got up and went over to Sam, who was spraying her hair in the mirror. "Listen, I expect this kind of crap from Diana, but not from you," she said in a low voice. "Emma is your best friend, so just grow up!" She marched over to the door and left.

Sam put down the hair spray and stared at

the floor a minute, then she swiveled around in her chair to look at Emma.

"Em?"

"What?" Emma said, sounding utterly miserable.

"I'm sorry," Sam said.

"I'm not," Diana put in. "Sorry if the truth hurts, Emma, but you have a squeaky little voice and everyone is going to laugh at you." She looked at herself in the mirror, turning her fedora on an angle.

Sam got up and walked over to Diana. "Get out," she said.

"I beg your pardon," Diana said huffily. "This is my dressing room, too!"

"Too bad," Sam said, standing over Diana. "Get out right now or I'll throw you out!"

"I'm leaving," Diana said, "but only because it's time for me to go give Kurt a backrub." She turned on her heel and went out the door.

Sam sat down next to Emma. "Look, I admit, I'm really jealous that you have a solo and I don't," Sam admitted. "I can't help it; that's how I really feel!"

"I know," Emma said forlornly. "But remember when you asked me to audition for this group with you? It was supposed to be fun. Remember? And now it seems like we're all just fighting all the time, and I hate it!"

"Yeah," Sam said with a sigh.

"Look, Sam. I love you," Emma said. "If it really means so much to you, I'll talk to Billy later about making this your solo instead of mine."

"You'd really do that for me?" Sam asked, wide-eyed.

"I would," Emma said softly.

Sam hugged Emma quickly. "You are a wonderful person, Emma Cresswell, and I probably don't even deserve to have you for my best friend."

"Probably not," Emma agreed with a small smile, "but you've got me, anyway."

"Emma, I want you to know one thing," Sam added.

"What's that?"

"You sing the hell out of that song," Sam said. "You sing it really, really beautifully, and the audience is going to love it tonight."

"Honest?" Emma asked, her eyes searching Sam's.

"Honest," Sam said.

"Thanks," Emma whispered. "Really."

"Thanks a lot," Billy said into the microphone as the applause died down after The Flirts had sung their eighth song. "We've got something really special for you tonight. A woman I love very much happens to be a hell of a songwriter. Her name is Carrie Alden—and we'd like to do her new tune for you tonight. It's called 'No One Knows Love.' I'd like to introduce you to a really wonderful singer who's going to sing it for you. She's real nervous so I hope you'll make her feel welcome—Emma Cresswell!"

The audience applauded warmly, and Emma walked forward from her place with the back-ups upstage. Billy kissed her cheek and handed her the microphone. The lights dimmed until Emma stood bathed in a pink spotlight, and Jay began the haunting melody on the keyboards. Emma closed her eyes, said a quick prayer— *Please God, don't let me ruin this. Let me be good.*—and began to sing.

> No one knows love the way that I do.
> No one knows how to play it so cool.
> So who can I trust? Where should I be?
> No one knows love, especially me.
>
> No one could hurt me the way that you do.
> You say that you love me, and I play
>   the fool.
> So why am I crying? And why can't
>   you see
> That no one knows love, especially me?
>
> So if I trust you, show you my heart,
> Will it be the end, or only the start?

Because no one knows love the way
    that I do.
No one knows how to play it so cool.
So who can I trust? Where should I be?
No one knows love, especially me.
No, no one knows love,
    especially . . . me.

Emma held the last note as Jay played the final, poignant melody line on the piano, and the song was over. For a moment there was silence in the theater, and then the audience burst into thunderous applause.

Emma was dumbstruck—she felt the applause wash over her like a wave of love. She turned around, looking for Billy, and he motioned for her to take a bow. As she bowed the applause grew even louder. *This is the greatest moment of my life,* Emma thought. *They actually liked me!*

The rest of the set went by quickly, and the audience made them come back for an encore. Finally it was over, and they all ran offstage.

Carrie had been taking pictures from stage right, and she hugged Emma exuberantly. "You were incredible! Fantastic!" Carrie cried.

"Once I got started singing I wasn't even nervous anymore!" Emma said, her eyes sparkling. "It was the weirdest thing!"

"Congrats, Emma," Sam said, hugging her friend. "Carrie's right; you were terrific."

Kurt walked up to Emma and stood in front

of her. "Can I add my name to your list of fans?" he asked quietly.

"It's not a list, Kurt," Emma protested.

"You were great," Kurt said, gently putting a strand of her hair behind her ear. "I was so proud of you."

Tears came to Emma's eyes. "Kurt, can't we make up? I hate all this—"

"Hey, Kurt, we still going dancing?" Diana asked, coming up to Kurt and taking his arm proprietarily. "I got the cutest and tiniest little skirt to wear. . . ."

Emma gulped hard and took a step away from Kurt.

"Emma, wait. It's not like that—" Kurt began.

"Just forget it," Emma snapped.

"It's a publicity thing *Rock On* magazine asked us to do!" Kurt pleaded. "All of you girls are invited—I put a note about it under your door. . . ."

"Gee, Kurt, I didn't get any note," Emma said in a frosty voice. She turned around and headed for her dressing room.

Diana smiled triumphantly, tossing her curls. Kurt threw up his hands in disgust and headed off in the other direction.

Sam eyed Diana suspiciously. "Why do you think Emma didn't get Kurt's note about this p.r. thing at the dance club tonight?"

"Gee, I wouldn't know," Diana said innocently. "Maybe one of the hotel maids saw the note sticking out from under the door and thought it was trash and threw it away."

Sam's fist flexed. She figured Diana had taken the note just to create trouble, and she wanted nothing more than to bash Diana's smug face in.

"Well, gotta motor and get into the shower," Diana said gaily. "I hate dancing with Kurt when I'm already all hot and sweaty—I'd much rather have him get me that way!"

Sam went to the backups dressing room and found Emma there changing into an oversized white minidress and white cowboy boots.

"Cute outfit," Sam said, slipping out of her jacket.

"Thanks," Emma said, sounding miserable.

"Hey, cheer up!" Sam exclaimed. "You were just a huge hit!"

"Yeah," Emma said with a sigh. She hung her costume on the clothes rack.

"I guess it doesn't mean all that much to you," Sam said carefully.

"Not right now, it doesn't," Emma replied.

"Well, as long as it doesn't mean that much to you," Sam began slowly. "I mean . . . did you mean what you said about giving me the solo?" she finally blurted out.

Emma turned to stare at Sam. "How can you be so selfish?"

"What?" Sam asked, looking bewildered.

"You told me you would. That's the only reason I'm asking!"

"It's not exactly what's on my mind right now, Sam," Emma said irritably.

"Okay, okay," Sam said. "It's just I think you should say something to Billy right away, before he starts to really think of it as your song. . . ."

"It felt great when the audience applauded," Emma said softly, staring into the distance.

"I bet," Sam replied.

"I don't think they would have applauded like that if I hadn't been decent," Emma mused.

"Right," Sam agreed, not at all happy at the turn this conversation was taking.

Emma was quiet for a moment. "I changed my mind," she finally said. "I want to keep the solo."

"You *what*?" Sam exploded.

"I want to keep it," Emma said defiantly.

"But you promised!" Sam protested.

"I didn't promise," Emma replied. "Besides, I was so scared then, but I feel differently now."

"Well, thank you so much," Sam said, her voice dripping with sarcasm. "That's the very last time I'm going to trust you."

"Come on, Sam. Don't be mad at me," Emma said. "I'm going through a really hard time with Kurt right now. And being out there tonight and hearing all those people applauding for me, well, it made me feel better."

"That's your reason for going back on your word?" Sam questioned bitterly. "Because poor little Emma isn't getting her own way with her boyfriend?"

"Sam!" Emma exclaimed, obviously hurt.

"Come on. What did Kurt do that is so terrible?" Sam asked. "I'm absolutely sure that he really did put a note under your door, and Diana took it on purpose."

"Maybe so, maybe not," Emma replied. "He's still acting like a total jerk. I mean, Sam, he actually *slept* with Diana last year! He broke my heart! And now she's all over him, and he loves it!"

"Well, you rejected him—" Sam began crossly.

"I did not!" Emma cried, hurt by Sam's accusation. "How can you say that?"

"All he wants to do is to spend time with you," Sam said, her irritation mounting.

"He wants to suffocate me," Emma corrected Sam. "And if he can't have things his way then he acts like a baby and flirts with Diana."

"You're the one who's acting like a baby because you can't get your own way," Sam replied coolly.

"You are not exactly the person who should be giving love advice," Emma said hotly.

"What's that supposed to mean?" Sam asked.

"I mean watch out or you're going to lose Pres," Emma said, gathering up her makeup from the dressing table.

"I'm in control," Sam assured Emma in a cold voice.

"Well good," Emma said nastily. "I guess it doesn't matter who you hurt, as long as you're in control." She hoisted her bag over her shoulder and marched out the door.

Sam stood there a moment, then she threw her lipstick across the room as hard as she could. *How could Emma lie to me like that?* Sam thought, enraged. *How could she tell me she was going to give me that solo and then just back out when she knows how much it means to me?*

She began to viciously throw her things into her carry-all bag when someone knocked on the door.

"What the hell is it," Sam yelled angrily.

"Wow, great mood," said Lauri Guzzepi, Johnny Angel's road manager. She was tall and large with long, straight brown hair and a mind that could juggle twenty problems at once and solve them all smoothly. She'd been on the road with Guns N' Roses, U2, and Sinead O'Connor. She was considered the best in the business.

"Sorry," Sam muttered, throwing her make-up case into her bag.

146

"Not to worry," Lauri said, "I've been abused by the biggies. Johnny asked me to ask you to meet him by the stage door after his show," Lauri said.

"He could ask me himself," Sam said crossly. She had actually been feeling kind of anxious because she hadn't even seen Johnny since they'd arrived in Washington.

"Yeah, well, he didn't," Lauri said with a shrug. "I'm just delivering the message."

"Thanks," Sam said. She packed the rest of her stuff and contemplated what she should do. *Maybe I really should get on the bus with The Flirts,* she mused. *I could spend some time with Pres. I kind of miss him. Or I could try and patch things up with Emma. Of course, she's the one who owes me the apology. Well, maybe I shouldn't have said the things I said about Kurt—but she made me so mad! Why does Emma always get just what Emma wants?*

Sam had a sick feeling in her stomach. She hated fighting with Emma. And she felt guilty, too, because she knew she had said things in anger that she didn't mean.

"Okay, so you're not perfect," Sam muttered to herself.

She pulled on her red cowboy boots and thought about Johnny Angel. *If I don't go with Johnny, maybe he'd just pick out some other girl. Or maybe he wouldn't. Maybe we're already a couple. I don't know, and it would be totally uncool to ask him. . . .*

"It's too complicated!" she yelled at her own reflection. Then she stuck out her tongue at herself.

"I know. I'll toss a coin," she muttered out loud, reaching into the bottom of her purse for a penny. "Heads I go with the band, tails I go with Johnny," she decided, tossing the coin in the air. It landed heads. She felt disappointed. "I can do whatever I want," she told her reflection defiantly. "And I want Johnny." She headed to the stage door to go wait in his limousine.

"You sure I can't convince you to come back to my hotel with me?" Johnny asked Sam, kissing her on the side of her neck.

It was three hours later, and Sam and Johnny had gone dancing at a very hip club where they'd immediately been whisked upstairs to the private VIP room. Sam acted like this sort of thing happened to her every day, but inside she was practically dying from excitement. Marky Mark was sitting on a couch across the room kissing a model Sam had seen on the cover of *Cosmopolitan*. Donald Trump was talking with a hot young actress at the bar.

And here I am, Sam thought giddily, *Samantha Bridges of Junction, Kansas, dancing a slow dance with rock star Johnny Angel. Yes!*

"This is wild, you know," Johnny said. "Me spending this much time with a girl who won't go to bed with me."

Sam shrugged, feigning a cool she didn't feel. "No one's forcing you."

"I guess not," Johnny agreed, caressing Sam's arm with the back of his fingers. "It's kind of unique."

"Mmmmm," Sam replied noncommittally. She kissed his earlobe lightly.

"Just so it doesn't go on forever," Johnny said. "Eventually the fun won't be so much fun anymore."

Sam's heart hammered in her chest. *Is he threatening to drop me if I don't sleep with him? What should I say?* "Since when do you worry about eventually?" Sam asked him saucily.

Johnny laughed. "Yeah, you're right." He kissed her and led her to the door and into the waiting limousine.

And he kissed her one last time when the limo stopped in front of her hotel. Immediately the chauffeur was there opening the door for her.

"Thanks," Sam told the chauffeur, stepping out of the car. *Boy, do I wish everyone back in*

149

Junction could see me right now! she thought to herself. She leaned her head back into the car. "Night," she called softly.

"Dream about eventually," Johnny said with a laugh, and his car pulled off into the late night.

I've got to talk this over with Carrie and Emma, Sam thought as she rode upstairs in the elevator. *Maybe I should just do the deed with Johnny. What am I really waiting for, anyway?*

Sam went down the hall to Carrie and Emma's room. She listened, and heard the sounds of the TV before she knocked.

"Hi," Carrie said, opening the door. "I'm watching a great old movie."

"Can I interrupt or should I go away?" Sam asked.

"It's okay," Carrie assured her. "I've seen it three times before."

"Where's Emma?" Sam asked, looking around the room.

"Don't know," Carrie said, sitting back down on her bed. "She went out about two hours ago and hasn't come back."

"I bet she went to that publicity thing after all," Sam mused. "I had a fight with her," she added sadly.

Carrie raised her eyebrows with surprise.

"Oh yeah? Maybe that's why she seemed so upset when she left here."

"Did she?" Sam asked anxiously. "I really wanted to see her. I acted like a brat." She threw herself down on her back on Emma's bed and stared at the ceiling.

"What happened?" Carrie asked.

"Well, we were backstage," Sam began.

She was interrupted by the blaring of an alarm.

"What's that?" Sam asked, sitting up.

"I think it's a smoke alarm," Carrie said, concerned.

"You think maybe some drunk guest just set it off?" Sam asked.

"I don't know," Carrie replied. "But we're on the twelfth floor—I'm not taking any chances." She walked to the door and felt it for heat. "It's not warm," she reported.

Just then both Carrie and Sam heard the unmistakable sound of fire trucks racing through the street, coming closer and closer, and stopping in front of their hotel.

They stared at each other, their eyes wide with fear.

"It's real!" Sam gasped. "We have to get out of here!"

Carrie ran into the bathroom and grabbed two towels, throwing them under the faucet and turning on the cold water.

"Come on!" Sam shrieked, pulling on Carrie's arm.

"Just in case," Carrie said, handing one of the wet towels to Sam.

They ran to the door and opened it cautiously. The hallway was filled with smoke. Sam turned toward the elevator.

"No, the stairs!" Carrie cried, pushing Sam in the opposite direction. "Stay low—there's more oxygen! Keep the towel over your nose and mouth if you need it!"

As they made their way toward the stairway the hall was rapidly filling with smoke. Carrie banged on every door she passed as hard as she could, screaming, "Fire!" hoping to wake people up. Sam began to bang on some doors too. People were running around in robes or under-wear, some screaming and panicking.

"Stay low!" Carrie kept yelling.

"Here's the door!" Sam cried when she felt it, for now the smoke was so thick that she couldn't see. She flung it open and she and Carrie headed down the stairs, as did dozens of other people. The smoke actually lessened as they went down, and the lobby was relatively smoke-free. Still they hurried out into the cool night air, happy and relieved to be out of the building.

"Everything is fine," a harried-looking man-ager was assuring everyone.

Another fire truck pulled up, sirens screaming. The fire fighters ran into the building.

"Doesn't seem very fine to me," Carrie muttered. She looked around frantically for the rest of their friends.

"The fire is in the cocktail lounge on the top floor!" a woman in a flannel nightgown was screaming frantically to anyone who would listen. "I heard a fireman say so! My husband is up there! They've got to get my husband!"

"Carrie?"

She turned around and saw Billy standing there wearing nothing but a pair of faded jeans. Carrie threw herself into his arms. "Oh, thank God!" she cried, hugging him as hard as she could. "Have you seen anyone else?"

"Kurt. Jay and Sly are over there," Billy said, cocking his head toward a crowd of people.

"Where are Pres and Emma?" Sam cried, clapping her hand over her mouth with fear.

"I haven't seen them," Billy said, his brow furrowed with worry. "Pres wasn't in our room when the alarm went off."

She stared at the burning hotel, tears streaking down her face. *Please, God, let Emma and Pres be okay. Please . . .*

Kurt walked mutely up to Billy, Sam, and Carrie, his face a mask of pain and fear. Wordlessly Billy put one arm around Kurt's shoulder and the other around Carrie. Carrie grabbed Sam's hand and held it tight. They stood there, hoping and praying as the fire fighters began to bring bodies out on stretchers.

"Lord have mercy, what happened?" came a familiar voice with a southern drawl from behind them.

They all turned around. There were Pres and Emma.

"Thank God!" Sam screamed and threw her arms around both of them, crying even harder now.

Kurt joined Sam and hugged Emma hard, wiping his own tears from his face. "Where were you?"

"We were out at an all-night diner," Emma said. "I guess we lost track of the time. . . ."

"Looks like we picked a good old time to not be around," Pres said, staring at the hotel.

"You two were out together?" Sam screamed.

"All night?" Kurt raged.

"Hey, save the moral indignation, we were drinking coffee, not rolling around on a water bed," Pres said.

"Is our whole group safe?" Emma asked.

"Yeah," Billy said, "They're over—"

"Diana!" Kurt exclaimed. "Where the hell is Diana?"

They all looked at each other, and no one said a word. They had all forgotten about Diana.

Until two firemen carried out the next stretcher.

And they saw Diana De Witt lying there lifelessly.

TEN

"The truth is," Sam said, as all the members of the band except Diana lounged around in the hotel lobby the morning after the fire, "even though I hate her, I'm glad Diana's okay."

"Me too," Emma added. She stole a look over at Sam, who had been treating her as if she were a distant, disliked relative ever since they'd gotten up that morning. *Well, so what if I spent a few hours hanging out with Pres?* she asked herself defensively. *I don't need Sam's permission to have Pres as a friend!*

"Me three," Carrie chimed in, "though it pains me to say so."

"When Diana got carried out on that stretcher," Billy remembered, shaking his head, "I thought she was a goner."

"She's lucky it was just smoke inhalation," Jay said gravely.

They were all quiet for a moment. They knew that one man had died in the fire that had started in the cocktail lounge, and two women were still in critical condition.

"I just got off the phone with Diana's parents," Kurt said, striding over to the group and taking a seat on the couch next to Emma. He was careful not to look at her. "They're flying in this afternoon."

"Good," Billy said. "Then we can move on."

"Move on?" Emma challenged him. "We can't just leave her here!"

"We've got a gig in Jersey in a couple of days," Sly reminded Emma. "The show must go on."

"But that's so cold," Emma protested. "She's a person!"

"Just barely," Sam pointed out.

"Look, I loathe her just as much as you do," Emma said, "but she's still a part of this band. And she got hurt in the fire because she was staying in this hotel on tour with this band."

"She got hurt in the fire because she was up in the cocktail lounge trying to pick up some guys from a touring company of Beatlemania," Sly said. "She told us that much herself!"

"You mean she wrote down that much," Carrie corrected Sly. "She can't talk."

"Yeah, right, but you get the general idea," Sly said. "You don't need to worry. Diana De Witt can take care of herself."

"I don't think it's right—" Emma began.

"Look, her parents are going to be here in a

couple of hours," Kurt said to Emma in a cold voice. "So just chill out."

"Hey, you don't need to go biting the lady's head off," Pres protested mildly. "She's just tryin' to show a little human concern."

"You don't need to defend my girlfriend to me. All right?" Kurt snapped at Pres.

"Well, dang, Kurt, she has a name. She's not just 'your girlfriend,' you know," Pres protested, his typically laid-back tone becoming steely.

"Butt out," Kurt replied in a menacing voice. "Don't go hitting on Emma just because Johnny is getting it on with your lady."

"Stop it, both of you!" Sam exclaimed, her face red with anger.

"You both sound like Neanderthals," Emma added. "It's disgusting."

"See, this kind of crap is exactly why I never did want to have chicks in the band," Sly fumed. "I warned you, Billy!"

"Okay, that's it," Billy exploded, his voice filled with rage. "We are talking about band business here, and that's it. You take your personal problems and you deal with them on your own time, is that clear to everyone here?"

No one said a word.

"Because if it isn't clear, or anybody doesn't want to abide by that rule, just speak up now and you're outta here!"

Again there was silence.

"Good, then we all understand each other." Billy took a deep breath and calmed down. "We were talking about Diana. Now, her doctor said she can't sing for at least a couple of weeks. Which leaves us short a backup."

"No problem," Sam said firmly. "Emma and I can handle it."

Emma nodded in agreement.

"If you have to," Billy acknowledged. "But Jay arranged all those vocal lines for three voices. And I don't want to go into the final gig at Madison Square Garden in New York with just two backups. All the Polimar execs will be there. What happens at that gig could mean everything to our careers."

Emma got an idea. She glanced swiftly over at Sam, then at Carrie, hoping they would both agree with her. "What about Carrie?" Emma asked hesitantly.

"Carrie?" Sam echoed incredulously. "I didn't know she could sing!"

"I can't!" Carrie cried.

"Come on," Emma said, "I know you can do it."

"No, I mean absolutely no, and that's final," Carrie repeated. "I am not singing on stage and that's it."

"She really can sing," Emma said to the rest of the band. She could see that some of them were interested in what she was proposing, but also that Sly and Sam were looking on with what could only be described as total disbelief.

"I know," Billy said.

"You've never even heard me sing!" Carrie protested. "I suck!"

"I heard you singing in the shower one day while I was hanging out waiting for you," Billy said. "You sounded pretty good."

"Meaning I have a tenuous grasp on a melody," Carrie scoffed. "That's about it."

"Doesn't sound good enough," Sly said.

"If she can carry a tune and do the dance steps, it's better than trying to limp along with two backups," Billy said, staring at Carrie. "But Carrie's got to make her own decision."

"I know you can dance, girl," Pres said. "That I've seen, myself. And you've heard the tunes a million times."

"Well?" Billy asked Carrie.

"Time out, time out," Sly said. "Isn't the band voting on this?"

"Not unless Carrie agrees to give it a try," Billy said evenly.

"Billy!" Carrie protested.

"Come on, Carrie," Emma urged her. "At least consider it."

Jay, who'd been sitting quietly watching this whole exchange, resettled his glasses on his nose and finally spoke up. "I think you could do it," he said matter-of-factly. "When we were rehearsing 'No One Knows Love' I heard you singing along with Emma. It was before everyone else in the band got there. You were decent."

Everyone looked at Carrie expectantly. Jay was in charge of doing vocal arrangements, and if he thought that Carrie's voice could handle the backup role, they weren't going to question him.

"You all really think I can do this?" Carrie asked warily.

"Yeah!" everyone yelled.

"Sam?" Carrie asked.

"I've never heard you sing," Sam said honestly. "But if you think you can do it and everyone else thinks so too, I'm all for it."

"Could I sing melody?" Carrie asked in a scared voice. "I'll never be able to learn harmony lines."

"Well, Sam sings most of the melodies," Jay said, "but I can do some rearranging."

Sam forced herself to smile pleasantly. But inside she was beginning to feel irritated. *Now I'm going to have to learn harmony parts, and I'm terrible at singing harmony, which is exactly why Jay put me on melody in the first place. But no one seems to be remembering that now,* Sam thought to herself.

"And it's only until you get a permanent

replacement for Diana or she comes back?" Carrie asked.

Billy nodded.

"Oh God . . ." Carrie said, throwing her hands over her eyes. "Okay. I'll do it."

"You won't regret this, babe," Billy said, giving her a hug.

"I regret it already!" Carrie yelped.

Emma got up, walked over to her, and hugged her. Then Sam got up too, walked over, and put her arms around both Emma and Carrie.

"Well, what the hell," Sam said, suddenly feeling glad that Carrie was about to join the band. "It's the three of us against the world, right?"

"It's going to take a lot of work," Billy warned. "You three ready to do it?"

The girls nodded.

"Good," Billy said. "We're leaving for Holmdel, New Jersey, in a little while. Kurt booked us in a day early."

"What for?" Emma asked.

"Because this place smells like a campfire," Pres drawled.

"That's right," Billy said. "So let's all go get our stuff, and meet out at the bus in an hour."

Everyone nodded in agreement.

"You guys," Billy said, looking at the girls, "you'll be able to rehearse this afternoon after we get there."

162

"Cool," Sam said. "Is Johnny Angel leaving today too?"

Billy gave her a look of disgust. "I don't know and I couldn't care less," he told her. "Try to remember whose band you're in, okay?"

"I was just wondering," Sam said, blushing. "We're all on the same tour," she mumbled.

"Yeah, well, wonder on your own time," Billy snapped at her. "Come on," he added to Pres, and the two of them walked away together.

"Be careful, Sam," Emma told her worriedly. "I really mean it."

"Billy's not mad at me," Sam scoffed.

"Yeah, he is," Carrie told her. "He really is."

Sam looked at their serious faces. "You don't think he'd . . ." She didn't finish her sentence because the thought was too awful.

"Kick you out of the band?" Emma finished for her. "I wouldn't push him if I were you."

"Hey, I ain't worried," Sam said blithely. "See you on the bus." She turned and walked to the elevator. The only evidence of how bad she felt was her shaking hands.

"Carrie," Sam remonstrated with her, "the move is turn-turn-kick-turn, not turn-kick-turn-turn."

"Sorry," Carrie mumbled. She, Emma, and Sam had been practicing the steps of their dance number for two hours, and Carrie was having a hard time with the difficult combinations in "Wild Child."

Emma walked over to the tape machine they had set up in an empty ballroom at the Holmdel Holiday Inn, and snapped it off.

"Let's take ten," she suggested. Carrie nodded gratefully.

"Uh, let's not," Sam said, looking at her watch. It was already nearly seven o'clock in the evening. "I've gotta meet Johnny at eight."

"I don't believe you!" Emma exclaimed. "Weren't we just talking about how you had to pay more attention to the band? Don't you think the dance steps are more important than your meeting Johnny again?" Emma slid to the floor and stretched out her hamstrings so she wouldn't cramp up.

"They're both important," Sam defended herself. "He called me before we left D.C. to tell me he was arriving tonight, too. I didn't know we'd rehearse this late!"

"I'm going to get a diet Coke out of the machine down the hall," Carrie said. "Be back."

"Sam, I really think you should call Johnny and cancel," Emma said firmly. "We've still got a lot of work to do."

"Oh, come on," Sam chided. "We can't work all night!"

"This is an emergency situation," Emma pointed out. "He'll understand if you cancel."

"Look, I'm not canceling," Sam said, "and that is that."

Emma stopped stretching and stared hard at Sam. "You're making a big mistake," she said softly.

"Oh, is that so?" Sam asked belligerently.

"Johnny doesn't care about you," Emma said.

"And you know, right?" Sam cried, flushed with anger. "Johnny couldn't possibly really like me, huh? Not me. After all, I'm not some perfect little heiress like you, I'm just some nobody from nowhere, so he must just be using me—"

"That doesn't have anything to do with it," Emma said icily. "Don't make this into some kind of class thing—"

"Everything is to you, isn't it?" Sam interrupted. "Emma Cresswell, the perfect heiress who never has to work a day in her life," Sam singsonged.

"I'm telling you because I care about you," Emma replied.

"God, I hate it when you get all superior!" Sam cried with frustration. "I would think you'd be trying to throw me and Johnny together so you could get your hands on Pres," Sam shot back at her.

"Oh, come on," Emma chided Sam.

"You think you could get them both, but I couldn't," Sam continued hotly.

165

"That is totally unfair!" Emma exclaimed.

"Yeah?" Sam asked. "If it's so unfair, why are you spending so much time hanging out with Pres?"

"Pres and I are just friends," Emma said haughtily. "You know that. Anyway, I'm amazed you even noticed."

"Kurt's noticed," Sam retorted. "He told me how pissed off he was."

"That's between Kurt and me," Emma said in a tight voice.

"Everyone's noticed," Sam continued, taunting Emma.

"Noticed what?" Emma asked, turning on Sam. "I'm not the one who's throwing herself at some guy just because he's a star. I'm not the one who's ignoring the band—"

"God, I can't believe you!" Sam exclaimed. "You wouldn't even be in this band if it wasn't for me! And now you think you can tell me what to do just because you lucked out and got a solo!"

"That doesn't have anything to do with it," Emma replied. "You better wake up, Sam, before you lose everyone who cares about you."

Emma turned on her heel and marched out of the studio.

Sam just stood there in a state of shock. How could things have gone so totally wrong? *Is Emma right?* she wondered miserably. *Is every-*

one mad at me? Am I really just throwing myself at Johnny and risking everything?

"Where's Emma?" Carrie asked, coming back into the room sipping from a can of diet Coke.

"Carrie, do you think Johnny really cares about me?" Sam asked, instead of answering Carrie's question.

"I don't know, Sam," Carrie said matter-of-factly. "You two never hang out with us together. I guess you're the only one who could answer that."

"I'm not sleeping with him," Sam said quickly.

Carrie didn't say anything.

"I just had a huge fight with Emma," Sam said bleakly.

"Not again," Carrie sighed.

"Why is everything so awful?" Sam cried. She slid down against the wall, put her face in her hands, and cried.

"C'mon Johnny," Sam said, snuggling against Johnny Angel as they sat side by side on the banquette of the Holmdel Jazz Club, "say yes."

It was nearly eleven that evening. Sam and Johnny had caused quite the stir when they walked into the club. Johnny's face, which had been on the cover of so many magazines, was instantly recognized. Sam loved the fact that people had crowded around, asking for autographs—why, someone had even asked for her autograph!

Sam had called Johnny and made their date later so she could stay and rehearse with Carrie and Emma. The three of them had practiced for another two hours without saying one personal word to each other. Sam felt a little better that she'd stayed, but Emma's taunting words still rang in her head. *Johnny doesn't care about you.*

As Sam had showered for her date with Johnny, she'd come up with a plan. She would get Johnny to agree that the two of them should do a hot dance duet during his set. That would prove to everyone how incredibly talented she really was, and would also show Emma and everybody how much Johnny really thought of her. She'd just sprung the idea on him.

Please let him say yes, Sam thought to herself. *Then everything will be perfect!*

Johnny laughed an easy laugh. "You, the girl who won't say yes, are asking me to say yes?" he teased her.

"It's a great idea," Sam whispered in his ear, as she draped her left arm over his shoulder.

"So you really think the two of us should do a dance number together at the New York show," Johnny mused, smiling as he considered the possibility.

168

"You know how good I am," Sam coaxed him. "We'd look great!"

Johnny looked closely at Sam.

"You think you can handle it?" he asked, putting his right hand on her fishnet-hose-clad thigh.

"Of course." Sam grinned. "I'm a professional, remember?"

"Yeah." Johnny grinned, flashing his perfect white teeth in that famous smile. "You're a hell of a dancer. I'll give you that."

Applause for the three-piece combo playing on the small stage at the front of the jazz club momentarily interrupted their conversation.

"So, is the answer yes?" Sam pressed. "We could do it to 'Too Hot to Handle,' don't you think?"

Johnny laughed. "Oh, you've already got the tune picked out and everything, huh?"

"Well, it's just a suggestion," Sam added hastily.

"I like a girl who knows what she wants and goes after it," Johnny said softly.

Sam held her breath.

"And you're right, we would look great together," Johnny continued. He stared at her contemplatively for a moment. "Okay," he finally said. "We'll include it in the show in New York."

"You're kidding," Sam said, shocked.

169

I never believed he would actually do it.

"You sure this is cool with your band?" Johnny asked her.

"Oh sure," Sam said, not knowing whether it was cool or not.

No matter what, I am not going to blow this chance! This could be my big break!

"Because I'm telling ya," Johnny said to her, "if one of my backups pulled a stunt like this—"

"No problem," Sam said easily. "It's cool. They need me. Besides, it's the last night of the tour."

"You're a big girl," Johnny said with a shrug, kissing her lightly on the neck.

"We're gonna be great!" Sam exclaimed, picturing herself doing a sexy duet number with Johnny in front of nineteen thousand screaming fans at Madison Square Garden.

"We'll work it up tomorrow and then polish it in New York," Johnny said. "You learn combinations fast?"

"I've learned it already!" Sam replied headily.

Johnny laughed. "Why do I like you so much?" he asked her.

He really does care about me! Sam exulted to herself. *He really does!* "Oh, I'm witty. I'm charming. . . ." Sam ticked off on her fingers.

"And I'm still not making love to you," Johnny reminded Sam.

"That could be a very temporary situation," Sam said in a promising voice.

"That's what I like to hear," Johnny said, and he kissed her until she couldn't even remember her own name.

ELEVEN

"Helmet?" Pres said, holding out a red crash helmet to Emma.

"I don't know about this. . . ." Emma hesitated.

She looked over at the huge Harley-Davidson motorcycle Pres had just rented and gulped hard. When Pres had called her room that morning suggesting they get away from everything and everyone for a while she had no idea his idea of a getaway involved whizzing on a big bike down dirt roads. They'd taken a taxi to the motorcycle rental shop, where Pres had calmly rented the biggest, baddest bike in the place.

"Hey, you've skied the double diamond runs in Aspen, right?"

"Yes," Emma acknowledged.

"You've flown in your father's jet during an electrical storm over the Andes, right?" Pres continued.

"I'm beginning to be sorry I told you anything about my life," Emma decided.

Pres smiled. "Well, what's a little ole Harley compared to all that?"

"That Harley is not little," Emma pointed out.

Pres climbed on the chopper and took Emma's hand, leading her to climb on behind him. "I'm a real safe driver, ma'am," he drawled. "Just wrap your arms around me and hold on tight."

Emma put the red crash helmet on and wrapped her arms around Pres's waist. Her breasts were pressed against his muscular back. *Why does he have to feel so good?* she asked herself.

Pres started the huge bike and it roared to life. They rolled out of the lot slowly, and headed toward the country. By the time Pres sped up, Emma was getting used to being on the bike.

"It's not so scary!" Emma called to him over the wind.

"Good!" Pres called back. Then he revved the bike and sped down a country road.

The wind flew through Emma's hair; the morning sun beat down on her face. "This is fabulous!" she yelled. "I love it!"

Pres laughed his rich, warm laugh, and turned the bike down a long dirt road.

No one knows love, especially me!

Emma found herself singing unselfconsciously, as loud as she could. Pres joined her.

No one knows love, especially me!

Emma held onto Pres even tighter. *This feeling is so incredible!* she thought. They passed fields and horses and barns, an occasional house, and felt surrounded by the expanse of blue, blue sky. Emma felt a sensation of freedom and lightness she'd rarely felt before.

After a while Pres slowed the bike down. "You ready to take a little break?" he called back.

"Sure," Emma replied.

They stopped at a grassy field and got off the bike. There wasn't a human soul in sight.

"This is fabulous!" Emma said, stretching her arms out as if she could embrace the entire world. "The air smells great!" She whirled around in a circle, inhaling deeply, as Pres watched her with an affectionate smile.

Emma took off through the field, running and skipping through the waist-high grass and flowers. "I hope you don't have any allergies!" Emma called gaily. When she'd run until her lungs felt like bursting she threw herself down in the tall grass and stared up at the perfect, blue sky.

"You look like an angel, lying there," Pres said, coming upon her.

"I'm not," Emma said seriously.

Pres dropped down next to her, leaning over her. "No, you're not," he agreed. He gently pushed some hair off her forehead.

"I . . . I . . ." Emma said, sitting up abruptly. Her heart was hammering in her chest. *It felt like he was going to kiss me,* she realized in a panic. *And I wanted him to do it! Oh, I'm a horrible person, and Sam was right about me!*

"Easy, Emma," Pres said, holding his palms up to show her he wasn't going to touch her.

"Are you in love with Sam?" Emma blurted out.

Pres sighed and stared into the distance. "I might could be, but she won't let me get that close," he said honestly. "She won't let anyone get that close."

Emma picked a daisy and twirled it around between her fingers. "And Kurt has just the opposite problem," Emma mused. "He won't let me breathe."

"Are you in love with him?" Pres asked Emma.

"Yes," Emma said firmly. She looked at Pres. "Which means I shouldn't be here with you."

Pres stared at Emma. "Girl, ain't no point in feeling so guilty about something that never happened."

"Right," Emma said in a low voice, staring at Pres's gorgeous face. "But I do."

"Well, if you're gonna go feelin' all guilty 'bout nothing," Pres murmured, "we might as well feel guilty 'bout something." He leaned over slowly, and softly kissed Emma.

She closed her eyes and gave herself up to the kiss. Before she knew it, she was kissing him back. He wrapped his arms around her and they sunk down, pillowed by the tall grass.

It was so wonderful that Emma refused to let herself think. But when a bird cawed loudly from above, it seemed to her it was calling "Betrayal! Betrayal!" and she abruptly pulled away from Pres. "We can't do this!" she cried wildly.

Pres sat back up. "You're right," he agreed. "We have to tell them first."

"No, no!" Emma protested. "We can't do this at all!" She scrambled to her feet.

"Emma—" Pres began.

"No!" Emma screamed, guilty tears flooding her eyes. "Sam is my best friend, and I'm in love with Kurt—"

"Emma, it's okay," Pres said firmly, grabbing hold of her shoulders. "It was just a kiss. That's all it was and all it ever has to be. Calm down."

"I hate myself!" Emma cried. "How could I do this?"

"Dang, girl, we didn't do anything! Chill out!" Pres exclaimed.

"Okay, okay," Emma said, taking a huge gulp of air. "I'm overreacting."

"Yup," Pres agreed.

"Everything is just so mixed up," Emma gulped, wiping the tears off her cheeks. "I thought we could just be friends. . . ."

"I think you're just as attracted to me as I am to you," Pres pointed out.

"I am," Emma admitted. "But I didn't think we had to . . . to act on it—"

"We don't," Pres agreed.

"Okay, so we won't," Emma said firmly.

"That's not gonna solve the problem, Emma," Pres said. "You can't clean the house by pushing the dirt under the rug."

"I have to talk to Kurt," Emma said in a low voice. "And you have to talk to Sam."

"I guess you're right," Pres said with a sigh. "This dishonest stuff is about driving me nuts. My life is beginning to resemble one of those soap operas on daytime TV."

"I know what you mean," Emma agreed, smiling weakly. She stood up. "And Pres, we can't be together. Whatever happens with Sam and Kurt, it just wouldn't be right for us to be more than friends."

Pres stood up, too. "Let's wait and see," he suggested. "I'm not willing to take that pledge right yet."

"Well . . ." Emma began, biting her lower lip in consternation. *I'm glad that's how he feels,* she realized guiltily.

"Come on," Pres said, holding out his hand to Emma. "We have to get back to band practice, anyhow. We'll just take this whole thing real slow, no sudden moves."

No more kisses, Emma vowed, taking Pres's hand and walking toward the bike. *I can't ever let myself kiss him again. I like it too much. Next time, I don't know if I could stop.*

Ring! Ring!

Carrie had just come out of the shower when she heard the phone in her hotel room. She wrapped a towel around herself and went to answer it.

"Hello?"

"Is this Carrie Alden?" a well-bred voice asked.

"Yes, it is."

"This is Celeste De Witt, Diana's mother," the voice said.

Diana's mother! Carrie thought with surprise. *Now, why would Diana's mother call me?*

"How's Diana feeling?" Carrie asked politely, sitting down on one of the beds.

"Better," Ms. De Witt said. "She's right here beside me, actually. She can't really speak yet or she'd be on the phone with you herself."

"I see," Carrie said. *No, I don't really see at all.*

"Diana had me look up the hotel's number on the itinerary she received, which is how I found you," Celeste De Witt continued. "I'm sure you don't mind."

"No, of course not."

"Diana wanted to know how the band is doing without her," Ms. De Witt asked.

"Fine," Carrie said. "I mean, it would be better with her, I'm sure—" she added quickly.

"Well, of course," Diana's mother said.

Carrie smiled. Celeste sounded just like her daughter.

"Diana is very concerned that the band will falter without her," Celeste continued. "Wait, she's writing me a note . . . she wants to know, is anyone covering her parts?"

"Well, yes," Carrie said. "Actually, I am."

Carrie could hear Diana's mother relaying the information. "Carrie?" Celeste asked. "Diana just wrote the words 'that's impossible' in huge letters on her pad."

"Well, she can write whatever she wants," Carrie said, slightly insulted, "but it happens to be true."

Diana's mother relayed what Carrie had said,

then spoke into the phone to Carrie again. "Look, if you have any plans to try and edge my daughter out of that band, I can assure you the verbal contract she has with these young men is completely legally binding—"

"I'm not trying to—"

"I'll have my lawyer look into this right away," Celeste said in a frosty voice. "And to think that Diana picked you to call because she thought you were the only one in that motley crew with any brains at all!"

"Look, Ms. De Witt," Carrie said angrily, "I don't have any designs on being in The Flirts. But let me tell you something. Everyone in the band is a lot happier now that Diana is there and we're here."

"Why, you jealous cow—"

"Gee, now I see that Diana's grace and culture are inherited character traits. Have a nice day," Carrie added sweetly, then she slammed down the phone.

She stared at the phone, half-afraid that it would ring again with a further tirade from Diana's mother. Finally Carrie stood up and walked back into the bathroom to dry her hair. She stared at herself in the mirror. "I am so lucky to have been raised by two reasonably sane people," she told her reflection.

Then she put the obnoxious Ms. Diana De

Witt and her equally obnoxious mother completely out of her mind.

"Okay, let's take it again from the top," Johnny told Sam. They were in a rehearsal studio they'd rented for two hours working on the dance number they'd be putting into Johnny's show in New York.

So far, so good, Sam thought, as she wound a few strands of hair around the rest of her hair to put it back in a ponytail. They'd already been working for a half hour, and it was the best half hour dancing Sam had ever had. Johnny was a really, really good dancer and so was she. Together, Sam felt certain, they were going to create history.

Maybe when the Polimar execs see us tomorrow night they'll decide we should be a duo permanently, Sam fantasized. *Then it'll be me and Johnny onstage and offstage. . . .*

"We'll take it from the bridge, on the double turn into the leg thing," Johnny said as he rewound the tape part-way.

Sam nodded. Johnny was a self-taught dancer of awesome talent, and he didn't know the technical names for the moves—but he sure did know how to do them.

They danced the bridge section of "Too Hot to Handle," Sam watching their whirling reflections on the mirrored wall. She pushed herself hard, giving it her all. She wanted to impress Johnny.

"Good," Johnny said, breathing hard. "Let me show you the finish, and then we'll put the whole thing together. There's a what-do-ya-call-it thing on the off beat—"

"Syncopation?" Sam asked.

"Yeah, right," Johnny agreed. "I'll count it off for you without the music first." Johnny showed her a dizzying combination of difficult and athletic steps. "Then I would finish with this," Johnny said, showing her a triple turn on the ball of one foot, into a spread-legged jump where he touched his toes and then landed in a one-handed push-up.

"Awesome," Sam murmured. She had watched him do these moves every night on the tour, but it still took her breath away.

"So, let's do that combination side-by-side," Johnny said, "but while I do the twirl-thing you do a flip-thing, then run and jump into my arms. I'll twirl you around by one hand and one foot, then we both do the final jump, and you land under me, face up, with me doing the one-handed push-up."

"*Under* you?" Sam asked.

"Sexy, huh?" Johnny asked. "I just thought of that."

"What if we both do one-handed push-ups?"

Sam asked, hoping that she actually could do one.

"Sam, it's a duet, but hey, it's my act," Johnny reminded her. "So we do it my way."

"You got it," Sam agreed. *I'm in no position to argue with him even if I do think having him practically land on top of me is a seriously awful way to end the number,* Sam thought to herself.

They practiced that section of the dance, and Sam had to work hard. *This is the toughest dancing I've ever done,* she realized. The harder she worked the better the duet got. After practicing for another hour without a break, they both flopped down on a mattress in the corner, probably left there for weary dancers.

"We're going to be incredible!" Sam said happily, catching her breath.

"You look very cute all sweaty like that," Johnny said, leaning over to lick Sam's cheek.

"Yuck!" Sam cried, but inside she was bubbling over with happiness. *Everything is going perfectly!* she exulted.

"So tell me," Johnny asked Sam playfully. "Tomorrow night after we unwrap this big number, we gonna go celebrate or what?"

"What did you have in mind?" Sam asked, smiling at him wickedly.

"Oh, say, a bottle of good champagne and you and me in the hot tub in my suite," Johnny suggested.

"Could be fun," Sam mused.

"Could be 'eventually,'" Johnny said in a low voice, reminding Sam of their conversation a few days before.

Sam took a deep breath. *Am I ready to go all the way with Johnny? Is he the guy who should be my first lover? But what if he's only hanging around because I'm a novelty—the only girl in history to hold out on Johnny Angel?*

"Johnny," Sam began hesitantly. "We've been spending a lot of time together. . . ."

"Uh-huh," Johnny murmured, nuzzling Sam's neck.

"And . . . well, I know you said it's different than last year on the yacht—"

"Totally," Johnny assured her.

"Because, well, I still haven't ever . . . you know," Sam said.

Johnny looked at her. "You're still a virgin?"

Sam nodded. "I know it's ridiculous, but—"

"Well, it's unusual. I'll say that much," Johnny stated.

"So, I would want to be certain that when I . . . when I decide to, uh, change that status, it's with someone I have a future with," Sam said nervously.

"I told you, Sam, I really like you. I always have," Johnny said.

"Yeah . . ." Sam said, her voice trailing off.

"If you want some kind of promises, I can't

make them," Johnny said honestly. "You are special, though, really special."

"Honest?" Sam asked.

"Honest," Johnny replied. "But you're kind of putting the cart before the horse," he added. "How would we know if we have a future when we don't even have a real adult relationship yet?"

"Meaning we aren't sleeping together," Sam said.

Johnny laughed. "'Sleeping' isn't exactly what I had in mind." He looked at her with amusement. "Listen, Sam. No offense, but if I just wanted to get laid, I wouldn't be hanging out with you, you know? There are lots of willing girls around. . . ."

"I know that," Sam said.

"So . . . the next move is yours," Johnny said. "You think about it."

"I will," Sam promised.

Johnny leaned over, put his hand on her thigh, and kissed her cheek softly. "You're special, Sam. Really special."

"Great candid!" Flash whooped from the open door of the studio, aiming his camera at them.

Johnny jumped to his feet. "What the hell are you doing here?"

"My job, my man," Flash answered him easily. He aimed the camera at Johnny again.

Johnny reached Flash in four long steps and

grabbed him by the collar of his polyester shirt. "What did I tell you about taking pictures of me without asking?"

"Hey, easy on the material!" Flash protested.

"How did you know where to find me?" Johnny asked Flash.

"Lauri, your road manager," Flash replied, as if Johnny were crazy.

"Lauri didn't tell you. I know her better than that," Johnny said.

"Well, I may have seen her daybook with the address of this rehearsal studio in it," Flash admitted. "But hey, *Rock On* loves those candids of the star working and sweating, my man. You *are* working here, right?"

"We're just playing around," Sam said quickly. She absolutely did not want Flash to know they were working on a number together!

"Playing around is right," Flash said with a leer.

"Look, fool," Johnny said, poking Flash on the chest with one finger. "We're two dancers, see?" He poked Flash again. "So we keep in shape by working out and dancing, get it?" He poked Flash even harder.

"You're bruising the goods, my man," Flash protested, rubbing the spot on his chest that Johnny had been poking.

"Give me the roll of film," Johnny said, holding out his hand.

Flash shrugged and opened the camera. He dropped it and fumbled to pick it up again, then handed Johnny the film.

"The only reason you are still alive is because I checked with Lauri and I know you gave her the roll with the shot you took of me backstage," Johnny said, tossing the roll of film in his hand.

"Oh, you mean the one of you and Big Red here swapping spit," Flash said innocently.

"Just get out of my face, man," Johnny said. "If I have to look at you one more time on this tour I'll make sure *Rock On* fires your ass. Got that?"

"Got it," Flash assured him. "You're the boss, boss! Sorry for the intrusion! Ciao!"

Flash backed out of the room and disappeared down the hall. Then he stopped, made sure no one was watching him, and pulled a roll of film out of his pocket. He chuckled softly. "The old Kodak switch-a-roonie," he said to himself. "Flash Man, you are evil. Fine, but evil!"

I'm going to puke. I swear to God I'm going to puke, Carrie thought miserably.

She was backstage at the Garden State Arts Center, far away from her dressing room, dressed in Diana De Witt's stage costume, about to appear with The Flirts for the first time. She wondered vaguely if her parents would be in the crowd. They knew Carrie was on tour with the band but had no idea she'd be appearing on stage. Kurt had had the white fringe outfits dry-cleaned, and now Carrie was squeezed into Diana's dress. She was at least a size larger than Diana and the dress was really tight. Diana's feet were bigger, and she had on two pairs of sweat socks inside the white patent leather go-go boots. All in all she felt totally miserable and absolutely certain she was going to make a complete fool out of herself.

"There you are!" Emma said, coming up next to Carrie. "I've been looking everywhere for you."

"I had to get away from all the hustle for a minute," Carrie said, her freezing fingers clenched into fists.

"Listen, I know how you feel," Emma sympathized. "The first time I went on stage with the band I thought I was going to die. But I didn't. And it turned out to be fun."

"I'm not you," Carrie moaned. "I should be down there dressed like a normal human being, taking photographs. This is nuts!"

"You're going to be wonderful," Emma promised. "Remember how great the rehearsal went this afternoon? You have all the moves down, Carrie."

"No one was watching me then," Carrie said, gulping hard.

188

"Carrie, Emma, let's go!" Kurt called to them.

"Oh God," Carrie moaned, grabbing Emma's hand.

Sam strode over to Carrie and Emma. "Come on, you guys, places!"

"I can't," Carrie pleaded.

Sam took Carrie by the shoulders. "You can," she said firmly. "You were fine in rehearsal. We left you out of 'Wild Child,' which is the only tough dance number, and I know you know the melody on all the backups."

"I won't even remember a word of the lyrics," Carrie wailed.

Sam led Carrie slowly toward the stage. "Yes, you will," she assured Carrie. "I know you can do this!"

Billy grabbed Carrie when he saw her and hugged her tight. "I love you," he whispered. "You're going to be great."

Sam and Emma half-dragged Carrie to her mike. Sam held Carrie's hand as the emcee introduced the band.

"Ladies and gentlemen, The Garden State Arts Center and *Rock On* magazine are proud to present . . . Flirting With Danger!"

The bright strobes lit up the stage and Sly hit his first drum riff. Sam dropped Carrie's hand after giving it a final squeeze for good luck. The band went into the opening licks of "Love Junkie."

"Ooh, ooh," Carrie sang. She knew there were monitors facing them, which meant that she should be able to hear her own voice coming back at her, so she'd know if she was on pitch. But everything was so loud and so overwhelming that she couldn't pick out her own voice at all.

When Sam and Emma turned sideways and swayed Carrie turned, too. Sam caught Carrie's eye and winked.

I guess it's going okay, Carrie thought hopefully. *Sam wouldn't wink at me if I was really messing up. . . .*

The whole set passed as if someone were fast-forwarding Carrie's life. Before she knew it, it was over, and The Flirts were running off the stage.

"It went great!" Billy said, grabbing Carrie to hug her.

"It . . . it did?" Carrie stammered.

"You were terrific," Emma assured her.

"Emma," Pres said, turning her to face him. "Your solo was purely magic, girl."

"Thanks!" Emma exclaimed happily. "It's because Carrie wrote such a wonderful song!"

"You two are really talented," Jay told Carrie and Emma.

Everyone crowded around Carrie and Emma. Sam was standing by herself, outside the circle, completely ignored. No one even noticed that she wasn't a part of the group. *They don't even care about me,* Sam thought. *I could be Diana De Witt as far as they're concerned.*

"Hey, luscious," Johnny whispered in her hair.

Sam turned around and wrapped her arms around his neck, kissing him hard.

"Mmmm, nice greeting," Johnny said.

"I've been thinking about what you said," Sam told him, "about tomorrow night after we debut our duet."

"Yeah?" Johnny asked.

"I think champagne in your hot tub sounds like a great idea," Sam told him fervently.

"Glad to hear it," Johnny said, his hands traveling down the small of Sam's back.

She kissed him again, and tried to blot out the sounds of her friends chattering together happily. *It doesn't matter,* Sam told herself. *I don't need them. I don't need anybody. Ever.*

TWELVE

"Hello, New York City!" Sam yelled at the top of her lungs, as she climbed out of the Flirts' tour bus.

They had just pulled into a space reserved for them outside Madison Square Garden in Manhattan—it was the afternoon of the final gig on their tour. There was a sound check in the Garden scheduled for three o'clock, and then the show itself was at eight P.M. After the show, both The Flirts and Johnny Angel would be spending the night at the famous Hotel Gotham, across the street from the Garden. For some reason *Rock On* had put them in a ritzy hotel for their very last night on the tour.

"Show's sold out," Kurt said to Emma as they got out of the bus.

"Great," Emma said, not looking directly at Kurt. She felt horribly anxious and guilty about Pres. *All I did was kiss him once,* she reminded herself. But even that seemed like a terrible betrayal of both Kurt and Sam. *You know you need to sit down and have an honest talk with both of them,* she told herself. But somehow the thought of admitting how terribly she'd acted behind her best friend's back was more than she could face.

"Yeah, the Big Apple, the place I was meant to be!" Sam bellowed as loudly as she could.

"Don't you ever just chill out?" Sly grumbled, walking by Sam.

"Spoilsport," Sam called, sticking out her tongue at his retreating form. *No one is going to rain on my parade!* she vowed. *I am in New York City, and tonight I'm dancing with Johnny in front of zillions of people. The Polimar execs will see me, and they'll realize I'm special. I'll get discovered, and—*

"Sam, you and me need to have a talk," Pres said, coming up next to her.

"If it's serious, I don't want to hear it," Sam said lightly. "New York is so cool, isn't it?"

Pres shook his head and went to talk to Emma.

"We'll talk later," she called after him. *Because if we talk now I bet you'll break up with me,* Sam added to herself. *Well, could you blame him, Sam?* a voice inside her head asked her. *You've only completely ignored him and flaunted your relationship with Johnny in his face this entire tour.* "I can't think about that now," Sam said out loud, brushing some hair out of her face.

She glanced over at Billy, who stood with his arm around Carrie, both of them staring at Madison Square Garden.

"Nervous?" Billy asked Carrie.

"Me? Nervous?" She smiled. "Why should I be nervous? Just because I'm going to be singing tonight in Madison Square Garden in front of a bazillion people?"

"I'm nervous," Billy admitted. Carrie took his hand and gave it a gentle squeeze.

"It's just that this gig means so much," Billy said.

"I know," Carrie replied.

"Everyone, listen up!" Kurt called to them. "Let's go check in at the hotel across the street. You're all pre-registered at the Gotham. Be at the Garden at three. Use the stage entrance, 'cause there'll be mega-security."

Together all eight of them crossed Seventh Avenue and headed toward the huge complex of the Hotel Gotham.

"Who's got tickets? Who's got tickets?" a young blond-haired teenaged girl kept repeating, as she walked along next to them.

"What's she talking about?" Sam asked Billy.

"Tickets," Billy replied evenly.

"For what?" Sam asked.

194

Now Billy couldn't hold back a huge grin. "For us."

"You mean she's trying to scalp a ticket for our show?" Sam asked, incredulous. Then Sam noticed more teens walking back and forth between the Garden and their hotel, repeating the words "tickets, who's got tickets?" It sounded to her like a magical incantation.

"I have a feeling it's Johnny Angel they're interested in," Carrie said.

"Oh yeah?" Sam joked. "Me too!"

Carrie shot her a warning look, but Sam just shrugged. Everything was simply too cool for her to bother being upset.

Tonight everyone will notice me, Sam said to herself. *And tonight Johnny and I will become an inseparable couple. Emma was totally wrong about how he feels about me, and I'm going to prove it to the world!*

Sam took a nap and woke up at two forty-five, throwing on some jeans and hurrying across the street to the Garden for the sound check. She gave her name to the guard at the stage door, and quickly made her way through a labyrinth of halls to the main stage. It seemed as if everyone stopped talking the instant she walked onto the stage.

Why is everyone looking at me so strangely?

195

Am I late? She automatically checked her Mickey Mouse watch.

Two fifty-five. Right on time. So why are they all checking me out like I forgot to put on clothes or something?

"Hi!" she called out, throwing her oversized bag in a corner.

Suddenly, Carrie broke from the group and ran over to her. "Oh Sam," she cried, putting her arm around her friend's shoulder, "I'm really sorry."

What in the world is she talking about? Did someone in my family die? Why wouldn't I have been called at the hotel?

Then Emma rushed over. "Sam," Emma said, "don't worry. It's going to be okay. It doesn't matter what you did with him."

No matter what I did with him? What is she talking about here? "Uh, what are you guys talking about?" Sam asked.

"Don't you know?" Carrie cried.

"Didn't you see?" Emma added.

"Know what?! See what?" Sam yelled. "You two are driving me nuts!"

"This," Billy said, crossing the stage to thrust a copy of that day's *New York Post* at Sam.

Sam took the paper from Billy. She turned it over. It was turned to page six. She looked down at the page. Then she thought she was going to be sick.

Right there, across the entire top half of page six, were two photographs, side-by-side. Sam was in both of them. So was Johnny Angel. One of the photos was the one that Flash Hathaway had shot early on their tour, where Sam and Johnny were kissing hot and heavily backstage after a gig. The other was a shot taken in a rehearsal studio, Johnny was kissing Sam on the cheek or the neck—it was difficult to tell because of the angle of the photo—with his hand resting intimately on her thigh. You couldn't tell in the photo that they were in a dance studio, though—all you could see was the mattress that had been on the floor in that room, so it looked as if the photo had been taken of the two of them in bed.

That's the picture that Flash took yesterday! Sam realized. *But Johnny demanded the film from him, and Flash gave it to him. I saw it with my own eyes! Well, big deal, it's a little embarrassing, but no big thing. This isn't going to get me down!*

"Listen, you guys, this isn't what it looks like," Sam explained. "We weren't in bed together. There was a mattress in the . . ." she let the rest of her sentence dangle. She didn't want to tell them she and Johnny had been rehearsing in a dance studio.

"It sure looks like you were in bed together,"

Sly called from across the stage, smiling smugly.

"Well, we weren't," Sam snapped. "Besides, I've obviously got clothes on."

"Sort of," Emma murmured.

Sam looked more closely at the picture. It was true that with the shot being sort of fuzzy, and with her wearing a flesh-colored rehearsal leotard, it kind of . . . sort of . . . looked as if she was naked. "At least I'm famous," Sam said, trying to salvage something positive from the photos. "Half the girls in America would kill to have their pictures in the paper with Johnny Angel!"

"Oh Sam," Carrie cried, "didn't you look at the caption?"

Sam shook her head. Then she picked up the paper again and read the caption under the two photos.

Rock heartthrob Johnny Angel, who plays the Garden tonight, has been stepping out with a backup singer (see photos!) from his opening act. No big thing, we know, but does Johnny's wife of six months know? She does now!

Sam dropped the paper on the stage as if her fingers were scorched.

"He's married?" she cried. "He can't be married!"

"Yes, he can," Jay said.

"I'll kill him," Sam seethed. She turned to Emma and Carrie. "You have to believe me; he didn't tell me!"

"Come on, Sam," Billy said to her. "If you're gonna play with fire, you're bound to get burned."

"But it isn't my fault!" Sam protested. "I would never have . . . have hung out with him if I'd known he was married!"

"Hung out with him?" Sly said maliciously. "Is that what you call it? That's a laugh."

"Come on, Sly, cut her some slack, man," Billy said.

Sam went running over to Pres. "Pres, I didn't know—"

"It ain't my business, babe," Pres said, turning his back on her.

"Don't any of you believe me?" Sam cried, whirling around to look at all her friends.

"We believe you, Sam," Carrie said. But she didn't sound very convincing, and when Sam looked at her she had to look away.

"When's he getting here?" Sam demanded. "I'll make him come admit to all of you that he never told me he was married!"

"Look, Sam. Frankly, it's your problem," Billy said. "It doesn't really have anything to do with the band, and I don't want it taking energy away from our show tonight."

"But we're more than a band!" Sam protested. "We're supposed to be friends! And friends care about each other!"

"Sorry, Sam, but you haven't been much of a friend to anyone lately," Billy told her coldly. "Now, let's drop it and get to work."

Just then, a blue-uniformed Madison Square Garden guard walked onto the stage.

"Flirting With Danger?" he asked.

"That's us," Kurt spoke up.

"Here, put these on." He handed Kurt eight laminated backstage passes, with the name of the band, Polimar Records, and *Rock On* magazine emblazoned on them. Kurt handed them out to the band.

"Don't let this affect your performance," Billy cautioned Sam again.

"That's really all you care about!" Sam said, wounded tears coming to her eyes. "That's all any of you care about!"

No one said a word.

The Flirts had finished their sound check and headed offstage when Johnny Angel, accompanied by the members of his band and his traveling entourage, swept regally into the Garden. Everyone in The Flirts kept right on walking, but Sam headed straight for Johnny. Johnny saw her, and came to meet her halfway.

"Hey babe," Johnny said as she approached. "I've missed you."

"Yeah right," Sam spat, "you've missed me. About as much as you miss your wife?"

Johnny just stared at her.

"Your wife!" Sam shouted again. She didn't care that everyone in both Johnny's group and in The Flirts was staring at them.

"What about her?" Johnny asked, mildly.

"Oh nothing," Sam cried, "except this!" She spotted a stray copy of the *New York Post* lying on one of the floor seats in the arena. She ran to it, grabbed it, opened it to page six, and thrust the photos of her and Johnny right in Johnny's face.

"I'll kill him," Johnny muttered under his breath.

"I'll kill *you*!" Sam cried. "You lying piece of—"

"Wait, Sam. You've got it all wrong," Johnny protested.

"Do I?" Sam asked. "Are you married or not?"

"Let's go talk in my dressing room," Johnny said, reaching for Sam's elbow.

"I don't want to go anywhere with you, you scum bucket!" Sam yelled. "Are you married?"

"Yes, but—"

"But what?"

"My marriage with Cyndi is a mess," Johnny tried to explain in a low voice.

The members of his entourage were deliberately looking everywhere except at Sam and Johnny.

"How can it be a mess? You've only been married for six months!" Sam shouted.

"It can happen," Johnny said. "Believe me. We're getting divorced. We have an arrangement—"

"An *arrangement*?" Sam screeched. "I'm the damned *arrangement*?"

"We're both free to see other people—"

"I don't do it with married men!" Sam hissed.

"You don't do it with anyone!" Johnny pointed out. "Jeez, Sam, chill out. Nothing really happened between us, remember?"

Sam felt as if someone had just punched her hard in the stomach. "It was nothing to you?" she asked softly.

"I didn't mean it like that," Johnny said, running his hand through his hair.

"Why'd you do it?" Sam asked, vowing not to let him see her cry. "Why did you lie to me?"

"I didn't lie," Johnny defended himself. "I just didn't . . . I didn't get a chance to tell you."

"How could you?" Sam asked.

"I was gonna tell you if things got serious," Johnny insisted. "But Sam, like I told you, things can't get serious when two adults are still just making out like kids. You know what I mean?"

Sam gulped hard, and even though she'd willed herself not to cry, a tear worked its way down her cheek. *I'd like to smash his face in,* she thought. *I wish the floor would open up right now and swallow me up. How can I face my friends ever again? Do I even have any friends left?*

Just then Flash Hathaway strode onto the Garden floor, three or four cameras slung around his neck.

"Excuse me," Johnny said to Sam, striding across the Garden to Flash.

"My man!" Flash said, reaching his hand out to shake Johnny's. "Good to see you!"

"Good to see you, too," Johnny mumbled, as he approached Flash. He stuck his own hand out to shake Flash's. Then, he coiled his right hand into a fist, and wheeled his arm into a huge right uppercut.

The punch caught the unprepared Flash right on the tip of the chin, and knocked him to the ground. Then Johnny walked up to him as he lay on the Garden floor.

"Don't hurt me!" Flash cried. "I'm just doing my job!"

Johnny took a huge leap, as if to land with both feet right in the middle of the prone Flash's chest. But instead of landing with his boots on Flash's ribs, he came down on top of one of Flash's dangling cameras. Everyone saw the camera shatter into about a million pieces.

"Hey, that cost a fortune!" Flash cried. "That's my baby!"

"Go to hell!" Johnny told him. "How'd those pictures get in the *Post*?"

"Don't know," Flash said weakly.

"I thought I told you to give Lauri the film," Johnny said, leaning down and putting his face inches away from Flash's fear-filled face.

"I must have gotten the rolls mixed up!" Flash defended himself.

"Yeah right," Johnny said. "And I suppose the same thing happened yesterday."

Flash smiled weakly. "Must have!" he said.

Johnny took another leap. He landed on top of another one of Flash's cameras. It crumbled under his hard-soled boots as if it were made of papier-mâché.

"Wow," Johnny said, standing back and surveying the damage he caused. "Who messed up your cameras?"

"Don't know," Flash replied, knowing he was beaten.

"That's the right answer, schmuck," Johnny hissed. He turned away and went back to Sam's side.

Flash gathered up what he could of his equipment and scurried off.

"Gee thanks," Sam said, when Johnny came back next to her. "That macho show just made everything all better."

"I didn't do it for you," Johnny replied.

Sam turned to walk away.

"Sam—" Johnny called.

"I don't want to hear anything you have to say," Sam said over her shoulder. Suddenly she stopped, and turned back to him. "Don't think you're gonna get out of doing that duet with me tonight."

"I wasn't planning to get out of it," Johnny responded. "It's on, if you still want to do it."

"Oh, I want to do it, all right," Sam said. "Because of you I am completely screwed with everyone I really care about. So all I have left is my talent. You understand?"

"You're a great dancer, Sam," Johnny said in a low voice.

"To borrow your phrase, 'that's the right answer, schmuck,'" Sam hissed. She strode a few steps away from him, then turned around again. "Just make sure when you introduce me tonight that you say *my* name, and not your wife's."

"Ladies and gentlemen," a voice boomed out over the sound system at the packed-to-the-gills Madison Square Garden, "please make welcome . . . from Sunset Island, Maine . . . Flirting With Danger!"

The whole band ran out onto the stage as the lights flashed, and right in front of the stage, a smoke bomb exploded. It seemed to Sam as if they were being hit by a wall of noise as they ran out, but it was only the boisterous New York fans yelling and screaming with joy because the show was finally starting.

I'm gonna show 'em, she thought to herself. And as she took her place at the mike alongside Emma and Carrie, she thought of the words of Polimar Records exec Sheldon Pincus, who had visited them backstage before the show started.

"Call me Shelly," the short, balding young exec had said. "I've heard you've had a great tour. We'll be watching you closely. Real closely, if you catch my drift."

Everyone had gotten excited, because Shelly was obviously saying that Polimar was considering The Flirts for a record deal.

That's what I have to concentrate on, Sam reminded herself. *Not that everyone hates me, not that even Emma and Carrie weren't speaking to me backstage before the show. I've lost Pres, I've lost them, and Billy is probably ready to kick me out of the band. I don't know if I can ever make it right with them. Sheldon Pincus from Polimar just has to notice me tonight. He just has to.*

As Sly began the drumroll that opened "Love Junkie," Sam came back to the present, ready to give it her all.

No matter how big a jerk I've been, I really want The Flirts to get a deal with Polimar, Sam thought. *They deserve it. And they all deserve a better friend than me.*

The Flirts moved into a forty-five-minute, nonstop rocking set that soon had the tough New York audience on its feet. They did their usual encore, but the crowd was screaming for more.

"Let's do it!" Billy screamed, and Sly hit the opening drum riff for Billy Joel's "The Night the Lights Went Out on Broadway." They had worked up the extra encore just for New York, on the hope—and prayer—that the audience would like them enough to keep begging for more.

"They love us!" Emma yelled as they ran offstage. She hugged Carrie, then Pres, then Kurt. Kurt held her tight for a moment, staring down into her eyes.

"Look out there!" Carrie cried.

The Garden was a sea of lit matches.

"Ladies and gentlemen, that was Flirting With Danger!"

New York had been a smash.

"Unbelievable," Emma said to Carrie, as they waited backstage after their gig.

"I agree!" Carrie said.

"Me too," Billy added, taking a bite of a sandwich he had made from the spread supplied by Polimar Records.

"How can you eat now?" Carrie asked him. Kurt had come backstage right after their set with a message that the whole band should be waiting in The Flirts' main dressing room, because he wanted to talk with them.

Billy shrugged. "I'm trying to look casual," he said.

"Yeah," Pres agreed with a grin. "Record execs come to chat up Billy-boy every day."

"Hi guys," Shelly Pincus said, striding into the room. "Great set, just great." He shook hands with Billy. "Call me Shelly."

"Okay, Shelly," Billy replied with a grin. "Glad you liked it."

"Liked it?" Shelly said, as if Billy were saying that he was glad that Shelly liked vanilla ice cream more than chocolate ice cream. "LOVED it!" Shelly exploded.

"Really?" Emma asked, unable to contain herself.

"We're talking killer, guys, really killer." Shelly looked around the room. "Everyone here?"

"Except Sam," Sly said, sounding disgusted.

"The tall redheaded singer," Jay explained.

"Gotcha," Shelly said, nodding. "Well, listen.

I wanted to tell all of you that you guys are dynamite. I mean, that's some serious music you make."

"Thanks," Pres said.

"So, guys," Shelly continued, "I'm gonna talk with my people, and we'll be back atcha in a week or so."

"Cool." Billy nodded his head, trying to stay calm.

"Great. Look, I'm gonna go catch the rest of Johnny's act," Shelly said, looking up at the video monitor in the dressing room that showed that Johnny Angel's show was underway. "You're welcome to join me."

Carrie, Emma, and Billy looked at each other.

"We're a little tired," Billy said.

"Hey," Shelly said, sweeping the few wisps of hair he had left on the top of his head off to one side. "Yo, I comprendo, babes. Well, ciao!"

Shelly hustled off toward the stage entrance, and Billy waited until he was gone before he reached his hand skyward to exchange high fives with Carrie and Emma.

"You think he's giving us a deal, man?" Sly asked Billy nervously.

"I think we got a shot," Billy said carefully.

"Believe it when we sign on the dotted line," Pres said cautiously.

"Pres is right," Billy agreed. "But . . . I got a good feeling about this."

"Where the hell is Sam?" Sly asked Kurt. "She should have been here."

"I don't know," Kurt admitted. "I couldn't find her."

"Forget it, man," Billy advised. He picked up his sandwich and took a big bite.

On the monitor, they could see Johnny Angel moving into his current number one dance/rap hit, "Too Hot to Handle." He was wearing nothing but a pair of baggy jeans, and his muscular torso shone with sweat.

"He may be jerking Sam around, but he is amazing on stage," Carrie said, watching him.

"You got that right," Billy said, watching the monitor intently.

Johnny led the audience in the rap hook to his big song.

> I'm too hot to handle
> My body's on fire,
> You better stay away
> 'Less you're ready to go higher.
> No doubt about it
> Burning out of control
> A five-alarm blaze
> Burning body and soul.

The crowd roared its approval. Then Emma, Carrie, and Billy saw something they wouldn't forget for the rest of their lives. Because Johnny

Angel yelled into the microphone, "Please welcome the very, very fine Samantha Bridges!"

Sam ran out onto the stage dressed in a pair of baggy jeans just like Johnny's, and with it she wore her tiny black spandex bra top.

"What's she doing out there?" Billy said, astonished.

"I'm going to go see," Carrie said, jumping to her feet. She hurried to the dressing room door, with Billy and Emma following close behind.

When they got out onto the Garden floor, they couldn't believe their eyes. Johnny and Sam were doing an incredibly complicated dance routine together—it was athletic, graceful, and unbelievably sexy all at once.

"When did they practice that?" Billy asked no one in particular.

"Go Sam!" Emma yelled, though she knew her friend couldn't hear.

And then the impossible happened for the second time in just a few minutes. Johnny had just flipped Sam over his back, and Sam landed on her feet, immediately going into a double spin. As she whirled around she never saw the lighting instrument break loose from its spot above the stage. It came crashing down on her head at an unbelievable speed. One second Sam was dancing, the next she was lying there on the ground.

211

"Oh my God!" Carrie cried, rushing to the stage.

The Garden hushed to a dead silence, as Sam lay on the stage with a pool of blood spreading around her head.

Johnny Angel and Carrie reached Sam at exactly the same moment. They both knelt beside her, afraid to touch her lest they somehow injure her more.

Sam never even knew they were there.

THIRTEEN

No change in her condition.

Emma heard the doctor's words echoing in her head. It was three days after Sam's terrible accident. The doctors at Beth Israel Hospital had sutured Sam's head wound, and she was not in mortal danger.

The only problem was, Sam hadn't woken up.

Six days later, she was still unconscious. The doctors didn't know when—or if—Sam would regain consciousness. She could come out of it at any moment, or she could lapse into a deeper coma. No one knew.

Sam's parents had flown in from Kansas, and her birth mother, Susan Briarly, had flown in from California. *Rock On* magazine was paying for everyone to stay on at the Gotham Hotel ("probably being nice to us because they're afraid of a lawsuit," had been Kurt's theory).

They were all spending most of their time at

the hospital. They talked to Sam, and played her tapes of The Flirts' music, hoping against hope that somehow, from somewhere, she could hear them. But she didn't respond.

Emma stared out the window of her hotel room at a driving rainstorm. *Will Sam ever be Sam again?* she wondered, tears falling down her cheeks. Like everyone else she had cried until she felt she had no more tears, and then she had cried some more.

"You want to get some breakfast before we go to the hospital?" Carrie asked Emma, coming out of the bathroom.

"No," Emma replied. She'd felt constantly nauseous ever since Sam's accident. Every bite of food she forced down tasted like sawdust.

"Me neither," Carrie admitted, sitting down on the bed next to Emma.

"Sam's mom called while you were in the shower," Emma told Carrie. "They already went to the hospital."

"Where's Susan?" Carrie asked in a dull voice.

"She spent the night there sleeping in a chair," Emma said. "It's as if she's trying to make up for giving Sam up for adoption or something. She's barely left the hospital since she got here."

"Well, neither have we," Carrie pointed out.

They both stared at the rain for a moment.

"It doesn't seem real, does it," Carrie asked rhetorically. "This is the kind of thing that only happens to other people. . . ."

"I keep thinking it's a terrible dream," Emma said softly, "and I'll just wake up. . . ."

"You know what one of the worst parts of all this is?" Carrie asked Emma. "Remember last year, when you and Sam went on that cross-country trip together and you stopped to pick me up—"

Emma nodded.

"Well," Carrie continued. "I keep thinking about how messed up things were then. I was so flipped out about school that I was stuffing my face all the time and making myself throw up, and you were upset about your parents and you were drinking too much wine—"

"And Sam got fired from her job dancing at Disney World and she didn't even tell us," Emma remembered sadly.

"Right," Carrie agreed. She got up to stare out the window. "I remember thinking that we'd all learned something so important, that we weren't going to keep secrets from each other any more, or judge each other—"

Both girls were silent for a moment.

"And here we are, keeping secrets, judging. . . ." Emma finally said.

Carrie turned back to Emma, tears in her eyes. "It just makes me wonder, about life, about God, I guess. Do you think there is any reason that we're even on this planet?"

"To learn?" Emma asked timidly.

"Maybe," Carrie agreed. "Maybe we're all supposed to be learning . . . something. Some kind of lesson." She stared at the carpet. "I feel like a real failure in that department."

"Me, too," Emma agreed sadly, thinking about the lies and half-truths she'd told. She looked over at Carrie. "But we can do better, I know we can."

"Sure, we've got another chance," Carrie pointed out. "But Sam might not."

"I believe she's going to wake up," Emma said fervently.

"I want to believe that," Carrie said.

"Then believe it," Emma cried fiercely. "If we believe it enough, if we love her enough, then she has to wake up. Doesn't she?"

They looked at each other, their faces etched with misery.

"When I was little and we went to church," Carrie said softly, "we were taught that God took care of everything, and if you were good, life would be terrif, and if you were bad, you got punished, and everything seemed to make sense."

"But it doesn't," Emma murmured.

"No, it doesn't," Carrie agreed. "I don't believe Sam is being punished right now, do you?"

"No," Emma agreed. She looked thoughtful for a moment. "But I do believe in the power of prayer."

"What, like you can petition God?" Carrie asked sharply.

"No . . . I don't know," Emma confessed. "I'm confused about it. I don't know if it's . . . God, or just the power of people who love that can change things—"

"So then why is it that sometimes no matter how hard people pray, innocent people suffer and die anyway?" Carrie asked plaintively.

"God, Carrie, I don't know," Emma said. "Maybe it's all just so . . . so big that we can't understand it—"

"And maybe it's all just a big cosmic joke," Carrie replied gruffly. "Maybe we don't want to face that because it's just too scary." She could feel the tears threatening to flow again.

Emma didn't say a word. She just moved over next to Carrie and silently took her hand.

A few minutes later there was a knock on the door. Emma went to open it.

Billy, Pres, Jay, Sly, and Kurt were standing in the hall.

"Hi," Kurt said softly, kissing Emma.

She leaned her head against his chest and he put his arms around her. All their arguments and misunderstandings seemed so stupid now, so unimportant.

"You guys ready to go?" Kurt asked.

"Yeah," Carrie said, grabbing her purse from the dresser.

Silently they headed down to the lobby. There was really nothing to say.

"How is she?" Emma asked Sam's parents, standing at the door of Sam's room in the hospital. Since the hospital only allowed a limited number of visitors in the room at a time, everyone else was waiting in the lounge. They planned to visit Sam in shifts.

"Her eyelids fluttered," Sam's mom said hopefully, looking up at Emma. "I'm sure I saw that."

Emma didn't say anything. She'd seen Sam's eyelids flutter, too. The doctor had told her it didn't mean a thing.

"I was just reading to her," Sam's father said, holding up a copy of the Dr. Seuss book *How the Grinch Stole Christmas*. "She always loved this book when she was a little girl. She said the grinch got a raw deal. . . ." Sam's dad's eyes filled with tears and he quickly turned his head away.

"We're going to go speak with her doctor again," Sam's mother said, getting up from her chair. Sam's father got up, too. "We'll be back in a few minutes." She leaned over Sam's bed and kissed her daughter on her pale cheek. "We'll be right back, Sam," she told her. Sam's parents left, holding each other up.

Emma sat down next to Sam's bed and stared at her friend a long time. Sam was so still, so silent. Was she there, inside somewhere?

"You have to be there!" Emma cried out loud. She didn't move a muscle. Emma gulped hard. *I have to be strong,* she told herself. *I have to reach Sam.*

"I suppose you think this is funny, Bridges. Well, it's not," she told Sam gruffly. "Although it is pleasant that you're letting me get a word in for a change." Emma got up and walked over to the window. The rain was tatooing the glass. Emma wished she could hit something, someone that hard. *Johnny Angel would be a good choice,* she told herself viciously.

He'd made one brief trip to the hospital, where he'd been surrounded by reporters, and after that he'd left town. Oh yes, he'd sent flowers. And that was it. End of story.

"Johnny Angel isn't good enough to wash your feet," Emma told Sam, turning back to her. "Okay, you're right. He's pretty," Emma said as if she were agreeing with something that Sam had said. "But, come on, Sam, Pres is pretty, too!"

Emma sat back down next to Sam's bed. She clasped her hands together nervously. "Sam, you were right, you know. I'm . . . I haven't been such a terrific friend, have I? Of course, you haven't been exactly wonderful yourself lately, either!" She took a deep breath.

"It's funny, you know. I got so caught up in being in the band, going on tour, worrying about Kurt—all my own stupid little problems—that I . . . I did some stupid self-centered things. And now . . . I want to apologize to you, Sam. Do you know how much your friendship means to me? I've never known anyone like you before. You make everything exciting and special. And you're the funniest person I know. You make me laugh, Sam. Before I met you, I hardly ever laughed. . . ."

Tears were streaming down Emma's face. "The truth is, I've always been jealous of you. Okay, go ahead and laugh. I know you wish you had money like I do, and sometimes you envy me—or whatever it is you *think* is me. . . . But Sam, I would trade all my money to be like you. You're not afraid of anything. No, wait, that's not true," Emma amended. "You're just as afraid as I am, but you never let that stop you. Never. And if you would just wake up now and tease me about this stupid one-way conversation, I'll never ask you for anything again. . . ."

Emma's sobs were impossible to contain. Her body shook with the tragedy of it all. But Sam just lay there.

"I'll sit with her for a while," Susan said from the doorway.

Sam's birth mother was short, plump, and going gray. She looked absolutely nothing like Sam. Right now she had red-rimmed eyes with circles so dark underneath them that they looked bruised.

Emma got up and grabbed some tissues from the dresser.

"Pres gave me this tape to play for her," Susan said, holding up a cassette. *"Johnny Angel—Heavenly Body."* It was Johnny Angel's debut album.

Emma just nodded and walked down to the lounge. When Carrie saw her, she put her arms around Emma, and Emma sobbed violently. Everyone else had tears in their eyes, too.

"I'd like to kill Johnny Angel," Emma cried viciously.

"It ain't the dude's fault," Pres said tiredly.

Emma turned on him. "How can you say that?"

"Because it's true," Pres said. He rubbed a hand across his blood-shot eyes. "If I thought killing him would help, I would gladly tear the sucker apart with my bare hands—hell, it'd be my pleasure—but it won't change anything."

Emma blew her nose loudly. "I just keep thinking, you know? Ever since Sam found out she's adopted, she's been going through a really

221

hard time." She bit her lip and forced herself to look at Pres. "I think she really loves you, Pres. She's just so scared to love anyone, to be that vulnerable. . . ."

Pres didn't reply. He just looked miserable.

"And we . . . we took advantage of that!" Emma cried. She looked over at Kurt. The day before she'd told him that she had kissed Pres. "I'm so sorry. . . ."

"We got ticked at her instead of seeing that she needs help," Carrie murmured.

"I should have made her sit down and talk with me," Pres said. "It's just not my style, but I should have done it. . . ."

"Wait a sec. Hold up, guys," Billy said. "We can't all be responsible for Sam, you know? She's got to be responsible for herself!"

Everyone stared at him coldly.

"I'm sorry," Billy cried, "but that's the truth!"

Emma stood up and wrapped her arms around herself. She stared at her friends. "All right," she said, "Sam has to be responsible for herself. But all of these games were going on. Nobody was confronting anybody." She caught Kurt's eye and looked away again. "It was easier to get mad and . . . and . . . wallow in self-pity than to really deal with each other honestly. . . ."

"Yo, Flirts, I gotta tell you—"

They all turned around to see Flash Hathaway, of all people, running toward them. He had on black leather pants and a flowered shirt open almost to his waist. They all knew that it was Flash's pictures that had appeared in the *Post*, and they remembered Johnny smashing his cameras.

"What the hell are you doing here?" Billy yelled.

"You'd best be running in the other direction real fast right about now," Pres said, advancing on him.

"Time out, big guy!" Flash exclaimed. "I just cruised Big Red's room, and—"

"Don't you go near her!" Carrie cried viciously.

"I'm trying to tell you, babes—she's awake!" Flash yelled.

Everyone stood there for a moment, rooted to the spot.

"She's—?" Pres began.

"Awake!" Flash repeated.

As if a starter pistol had gone off, they all ran down the corridor to Sam's room and crowded around her door. A doctor, her parents, and her birth mother were all by her bed.

And Sam's eyes were open.

She spotted Flash standing in the doorway. "It really *was* you!" she said in a weak voice. "I figured I died and didn't get accepted into heaven, so . . ."

Everyone laughed, even Flash.

"Flash in the flesh!" Flash yelled.

"We're very happy to see you," the gray-haired doctor told Sam, looking into her eyes with a small light. "How are you feeling?"

"My head hurts," Sam said, reaching up to the side of her head that was covered in bandages.

"You got conked pretty good," the doctor said. "Do you remember what happened?"

Sam furrowed her brow. "I was dancing with Johnny, wasn't I? And then . . . that's all I remember!"

"That's about it," the doctor said with a smile. "I'll leave you with your friends and family for a few minutes, but then everyone has to clear out so I can examine you." He grinned at Sam. "Welcome back."

Sam's mother took her hand. "Oh, Sam . . ." she said, overcome with emotion.

Sam's friends crowded around her bed. Susan Briarly ended up outside the tight circle, standing in the doorway. Only Emma saw her walk silently away.

"You're all here!" Sam said. "I feel like Dorothy at the end of *The Wizard of Oz*!"

"We love you, Sam," Sam's dad said, gulping hard.

"We all love you," Carrie added fervently.

A cloud passed over Sam's face. "Oh God, I was so terrible to everyone. . . ."

Pres leaned over and gently kissed Sam's cheek. "Yeah, you suck, girl, but I love you anyway," Pres said gruffly.

"Do you mean that?" Sam asked in a small voice.

"I'm willing to work on it if you're willing to work on it," Pres said. "But you got to be willing . . ."

"I'm scared," Sam whispered. "That's the truth."

"You ought to get conked on the head more often," Sly remarked. "It's making you turn honest!"

Jay bashed him in the arm.

Sam looked at Pres. "I don't deserve a boyfriend like you," Sam said, gulping hard.

"I'm not so perfect," Pres said, catching Emma's eye. "But I guess there are some things we both needed to learn the hard way."

"I guess," Sam agreed. Her face searched out Emma's. "You know, I had the strangest dream. I dreamt that you told me you were jealous of me! And you said you'd gladly give up all your money if you could only be more like me. Isn't that ridiculous?"

She heard me! Emma exulted. *Thank you, God. She actually heard me!* "Stupidest thing I ever heard," Emma agreed, tears streaming down her happy face. *There'll be time enough to tell her the truth,* Emma thought. *And this time, the truth is exactly what I'm going to tell.*

Emma caught Carrie's eye and smiled.

Why, Emma really did say those things! Carrie realized. *And somehow, from wherever Sam was, she heard her.* "No one could be like you, Sam," Carrie said. "When they made you they broke the mold."

"It's a good thing," Flash said from where he was standing near the wall. "No offense, Big Red, but the world couldn't handle two of you."

Everyone turned to look at him.

"Hey, I'm outta here!" he exclaimed, heading for the door. He looked back at Sam. "Glad you're okay, babe," he mumbled before scurrying down the hall.

Sam looked around her, at her parents and all her friends. *So many great people care about me,* she realized, *and I've been so unfair to them. . . .* "You guys don't hate me?" Sam asked.

"Hey, all for one and one for all, remember?" Emma asked Sam softly.

"Yeah, but lately I've been sort of all for me," Sam admitted.

"Well, I guess we'll have to work on that," Carrie said, smiling at her friend.

"I guess we will," Sam agreed. She took in the

dear faces—her parents, the band members, and Emma and Carrie—the very best friends anybody ever had.

"Let's face it," Sam said, "Big Red is one lucky babe."

And as Sam smiled up at all of them, she realized how very true that was.

THE SUNSET ISLAND SERIES
by Cherie Bennett

Emma, Sam, and Carrie are different in every way. When they spend the summer working as au pairs on a resort island, they quickly become allies in adventure!

SUNSET ISLAND
0 863 69800 X/£3.50

Emma, Carrie, and Sam set out for a fantastic summer of fun and independence on Sunset Island. The three get jobs working for terrific families, and the guys on the island are cuter than *any* at home. This is definitely a summer none of them will forget!

SUNSET KISS
0 863 69805 0/£3.50

Carrie's decided that this is it – the summer she finally shakes off her boring "girl-next-door" image forever in order to win the boy of her dreams. But when she sneaks out on the children she's caring for and gets caught by the police in a very compromising position, she discovers that boring may not be so bad after all!

SUNSET DREAMS
0 863 69810 7/£3.50

Sam thinks she's got what it takes to be a successful model, so when a photographer agrees with her, she's in seventh heaven. He wants her to go away with him for the weekend. It's up to her friends to stop her – before she makes the biggest mistake of her life!

SUNSET FAREWELL
0 863 69815 8/£3.50

Emma just can't believe what is going on right underneath her nose! It seems Diana, her worst enemy, is back on Sunset Island, and she's gone beyond being snotty and rude. She's gone after Emma's boyfriend, Kurt. But Kurt thinks Diana's great and Emma's *too* touchy ...

SUNSET REUNION
0 863 69820 4/£3.50

Sam lands a job as a dancer, Emma's turning over a new leaf and Carrie manages to get backstage passes to one of the hottest concerts of the year. Soon, they find themselves to be the centre of attention when they're invited to hang out on rock star Graham Perry's yacht. Thrown into an adult world, all three friends have to make big decisions about who they want to be.

SUNSET SECRETS
0 863 69801 8/£3.50

It's winter, and Carrie, Emma and Sam are on the road to Sunset Island for a mega pre-season party. Everyone's going to be there, including Kurt and Billy. But their journey is not without problems. And what is everyone going to think when the girls turn up with their new admirers in tow?

SUNSET HEAT
0 863 69806 9/£3.50

Sam is hired by a talent scout to dance in a show in Japan. Unfortunately, Emma and Carrie don't share her enthusiasm. No one really knows if this is on the up and up, especially after her fiasco with the shifty photographer last summer. But Sam is determined to go despite her friends . . .

SUNSET PROMISES
0 863 69876 X/£3.50

Carrie receives a lot of attention when she shows her photos at the Sunset Gallery. She is approached by a publisher who wants her to do a book of pictures of the island. But when Carrie photos the entire island, she discovers a part of Sunset Island that tourists never see . . .

SUNSET SCANDAL
0 863 69881 6/£3.50

Emma has started to see Kurt again, and everything's going great . . . until Kurt is arrested as the suspect in a rash of robberies! He has no alibi, and things look pretty bad. Then, Emma befriends a new girl on the island who might be able to help prove Kurt's innocence.

SUNSET WHISPERS
0 863 69812 3/£3.50

Sam is shocked to find out she is adopted. She's never needed her friends more than when her birth mother comes to Sunset Island to meet her. And to add to the chaos, Sam and Emma, along with the rest of the girls on the island, are auditioning to be back-up in the rock band *Flirting with Danger*.

SUNSET PARADISE
0 863 69817 4/£3.50

When Emma wins the Paradise Swimwear trip to Paradise Island in the Bahamas, life really takes an upward turn for the three friends. Everything is going great! There are no curfews, no kids to take care of and lots of hunky guys to hang out with on the beach. And when Sam is spotted by a top choreographer, this really could be the break she needs to make it into the big time.

SUNSET SURF
January 1995/0 863 69898 0/£3.50

Sam's been invited back to San Francisco by her real mother. She can't decide whether to accept, until it turns out Carrie's going there on a photo shoot. Emma's at a loose end, so she tags along too but it suddenly doesn't seem such a good idea when she falls for Sam's new found brother. Just what is she going to tell Kurt?

SUNSET DECEPTIONS
February 1995/0 863 69804 2/£3.50

When Carrie's Hispanic friend, Raymond Saliverez, shows up on the island, he's there on a mission. His student visa is running out fast and he needs a green card in order to continue his studies. He daren't return to his own country and there's only one way to get legal: for Carrie to say yes to his marriage proposal. But she's already dating Billy, and he won't be pleased when he finds out what's going on.

SUNSET ON THE ROAD

March 1995/0 863 69955 3/£3.50

It's adventure on the move as the girls set out on tour with Sunset Island's funkiest band, Flirting with Danger. Emma and Sam are the backing singers, Kurt's on the crew, and Carrie's come along to do a documentary about them. Surely even bitchy Diana De Witt can't ruin this ride – or can she?

To order any of the **Sunset Island** books, please enclose a cheque or postal order made payable to **Virgin Publishing Ltd**, to the value of the books you have ordered plus postage and packing costs as follows:

> UK and BFPO – 70p for the first book, 50p for the second book, and 30p for each subsequent book to a maximum of £3.00;
> Overseas (including Republic of Ireland) – £2.00 for the first book, £1.00 for the second book, and 50p for each subsequent book.

Send to: **Cash Sales, Virgin Publishing Ltd, 332 Ladbroke Grove, London W10 5AH**

If you would prefer to pay by VISA or ACCESS/ MASTERCARD, please write your card number here.

_____

expiry date_____

Please allow up to 28 days for delivery

Name_____

Address_____

_____Post Code_____